"CRAZY SON OF A BITCH!" KATE SCREAMED.

Bright sparks flashed in the night as the men in the back seat of the lead car began firing at the Kenworth. Slugs whined off the cab. Barry lowered his window, leaned out, and gave the sedan a full clip from his Uzi.

"Ram him!" Barry yelled.

Kate shifted and plowed into the rear of the car. Sparks flew as the rear tires of the sedan blew out and the frame and bumper began dragging the concrete. The sedan spun crazily in the road and then went over the side. Kate and Barry could hear the screams of the men in the doomed vehicle.

The car turned end over end and was soon lost from sight in the misty night.

"One down," Barry muttered.

Dear friends,

I've had so many requests for the return of the RIG WARRIOR series that I've finally persuaded my publisher to bring them back. Here they are—one each month, in July, August, and September!

Barry Rivers has always been a favorite among the heroes I've created. Like many an independent thinker, Barry doesn't like to wait for the slow wheels of justice to turn, so he takes matters into his own hands. He travels alone—with his trusty partner, Dog, beside him in his eighteen-wheeler.

I hope you enjoy the RIG WARRIOR books. If you do—or even if you don't—I'd be happy to hear from you. You can write to me care of my publisher, or e-mail me at *dogcia@aol.com*

Happy reading!
Bill Johnstone

RIG WARRIOR

William W. Johnstone

Pinnacle Books
Kensington Publishing Corp.

http://www.pinnaclebooks.com

PINNACLE BOOKS are published by

Kensington Publishing Corp.
850 Third Avenue
New York, NY 10022

First Printing: May, 1987
First Pinnacle Printing: July, 2000
10 9 8 7 6 5 4 3 2

Printed in the United States of America

This book is dedicated to Steve and Barbara Benson, good friends of mine. Without their help, this book would not have been possible. I would also like to thank Karen and Edwin Smith, Gerald B. Simpson, W. J. and Mary Lopez, and all the thousands of truck drivers rolling throughout this country. It's about time somebody recognized their efforts!

1

He didn't think of his dad every time he saw an eighteen-wheeler; if he did that, he'd be thinking of his dad all the time and would never get any work done.

It was when he was tired from battling the bureaucrats, or looking at figures all day, or trying to convince some general who never should have risen above the rank of private that whatever idea the general had come up with sucked . . . that's when Barry would lean back in his chair in his Washington office and look out the window. More than likely there'd be an eighteen-wheeler on the not-too-distant interstate, twin chrome stacks gleaming in the sun as it hurtled along the road. Sometimes he'd hear the lonesome sounds of air horns drifting to him, through the glass and steel and concrete of his office.

And he'd think of his dad.

Then he'd have to shake himself like a big shaggy dog,

drag himself out of his daydreaming, and come back to reality.

Sometimes he'd make it back and sometimes he wouldn't.

And sometimes he'd feel guilty.

He had to make plans to go back to New Orleans and spend some time with his dad. He hadn't seen him in over two years. He'd just been so damn busy. Oh, he talked with his dad every two or three weeks. But that wasn't the same as *seeing* him.

And, come to think of it, the last four or five talks they'd had . . . well, he thought he'd detected something odd-sounding in his father's voice. Maybe a touch of strain. Fear? Yeah, maybe. First time he'd thought of that word. But maybe fear was it.

Barry Rivers's father afraid of something?

Barry chuckled at that. He couldn't imagine Big Joe Rivers being afraid of the devil himself.

But the old man was sixty now; and age does funny things to a person.

Ah, hell! Come on, Barry. You're imagining things. Reading something into the old man's voice that isn't really there.

Or was he?

"Barry?" his secretary's voice brought him out of his musings.

He looked at the woman. Maggie. His secretary, his Mom-figure. Sixty years old and looking fifty. Barry could not imagine his office running without her. His own mother had died when Barry was ten. He could just remember her.

For sure, Barry clung to his musings, his father had to be lonesome.

"Maggie. What'd I forget?"

"Nothing that I know of. You need a vacation, Barry. More and more I look in here and see you a thousand miles away."

Barry waved at the neat piles of paper on his desk. "Tell me how I take a vacation?"

Air horns sounded on the interstate. Barry looked out the window. A Peterbilt pulling a flatbed. Right behind the Peterbilt, a White Tall Sleeper pulling a dry van.

"Barry!" Maggie said.

Barry looked back at her, a sheepish grin on his face. He was forty and didn't look it. Five feet ten inches. One hundred and seventy-five hard pounds. Barry kept himself hard by working out one hour each day in his home gym, and several hours a day on the weekends—when time permitted it. And he usually made time permit it. He'd kicked cigarettes several years back, and still marveled at how good food tasted since he'd quit smoking. Black hair still mostly free of gray, except around the temple area, and deep blue eyes. Handsome in a rugged sort of way. He had never been called a pretty boy. His chin was square and solid.

"Damn gypsy," Maggie fussed at him.

"Cajun," Barry corrected, although he knew she was referring to his truck-driving youth and not his heritage.

His heritage had given him a volatile temper: Irish on his mother's side, Cajun French on his father's side.

He had learned over the years to control his ragin' Cajun temper, but he could still fly off the handle and do it so fast the person it was directed toward usually had the hell scared out of them.

"Barry," Marrie gently chided him. "Your work is caught up. Go home for a while."

"Is that an order, General?"

"Damn sure is, Colonel," she popped back.

He was kidding her about the General bit, but she wasn't about the Colonel bit.

He'd graduated from high school in New Orleans at sixteen, top of his class. Two years in college at Lafayette, working during the summers driving for his dad. And then, bored, he'd left school and joined the Army. Jump school, Ranger school, and then into OCS. From OCS he'd headed for the Special Warfare schools at Fort Bragg. Seventh Special Forces. Eighteen months later, he was a captain, CO of an A-Team in Southeast Asia. He spent four years in Vietnam, and the promotions hit him as fast as the lead his body soaked up during that time. Three times wounded, three times promoted. But the events were in no way related.

When he got out, he stayed in the Reserves while finishing his education, driving a rig for his father on the weekends and during college breaks.

The driving had been fun; college had not been. He was a decorated war hero out of an unpopular war. And while the antiwar sentiment had never been strong in Louisiana—Southern boys have a tendency to be very patriotic—there was enough antiwar sentiment to make him uncomfortable.

It was in Lafayette he'd met Julie.

She was definitely antiwar. From New Hampshire. Old family with lots of money. Bluenoses. Bluebellies, Barry liked to kid her, until he discovered she had practically no sense of humor when it came to the War Between the States, as he called it. The Civil War, as she referred to it.

Opposites attract, and they got married. Very large mistake. The marriage lasted through the sometimes-stormy, oftentimes-silent, cold years. Julie left him in '76. Happy bicentennial, Barry. She'd taken the two kids that weekend he'd been doing his Reserve bit and hauled ass back to New Hampshire. Lawyers handled the rest of it.

By the time the breakup came, Barry had moved the family to Washington and was working as a civilian consultant to the U.S. Army. Weapons expert. He'd traveled a lot. Julie had bitched a lot—and had turned the kids against him. Barry Junior and Missy were coming out of that now, but it had taken years.

Maybe he did need a vacation. Hell, he knew he did.

As if reading his mind, Maggie said, "But not this week, Barry. Tie up all the loose ends, and by Friday, you'll be clear for a month. Nothing on the agenda the rest of the guys can't handle."

He smiled at her. "What would I do without you, Maggie?"

"Get to work, Barry. We've got a lot to do this week."

Maggie stuck her head into his office. "It's five-thirty, Barry."

He couldn't believe it. He glanced at his wristwatch. Sure was five-thirty. "Rest of the people gone?"

"About thirty minutes ago. I'm leaving now, unless there's anything else."

He shook his head. "No. I'll just finish up these reports and then lock everything up. See you in the morning."

He listened to her footsteps fade, then the sounds of the door closing, the dead-bolt lock engaging. There'd been a lot of break-ins around here recently, and people were becoming more security-conscious than ever.

Barry's consultant firm was located in Maryland, about a block and a half from the Beltway. At first he had located in D.C. proper, but after two years of fighting the congestion of that myriad of screwed-up streets, he tossed in the towel and moved to Maryland.

It had been a good move.

He looked at the stacks of paper on his huge desk and sighed. He had made a dent in them, but it was going to be tough to get away Friday afternoon.

He checked his day's appointments to be certain he had not scheduled anything for that evening. Good. Nothing. He didn't feel like seeing anyone. And didn't feel like going to his apartment for dinner. He'd call for something. Maybe a pizza; have it delivered and work 'til about ten or so. By that time he'd be tired enough to hit the sheets and get a good night's sleep.

Then he decided to call his dad. It had been several weeks since he'd spoken with him. He punched the speed-caller and listened to the phone ring at his father's house. No answer. He redialed, calling his dad's office at the terminal. Somebody was there twenty-four hours a day.

Rivers Trucking employed thirty-five full-time drivers, in addition to the office workers, dispatchers, mechanics, and other workers.

But there was no answer.

Now, that was weird.

Well, the office workers would have gone home by now, and maybe the dispatcher was taking a leak. He'd try again later.

He leaned back in his padded leather chair and smiled. Hell, Big Joe was probably out on the road. He knew his dad had just bought a couple million dollars' worth of new equipment; Kenworth conventionals. The W900Bs. And he knew his dad disliked office work vehemently; and he'd have his own tractor, which no one would dare touch except Big Joe. He'd have it outfitted to his liking; the interior of the cab probably done in red leather or vinyl, hand-sewn, with a soft, full headliner. Air Cushion seat, orthopedically shaped and padded to best support, properly, the human body at work. Big Joe was worth a lot of money, but he was a driver at heart, and he would have the best for his people. Big Joe paid his people well, and demanded the max from them.

Barry wondered how many women he had working for him. Big Joe had gritted his teeth and done a lot of bitching when women first went to work driving, and not all of them made it with Rivers Trucking. Those that did were top-of-the-line truckers, and they wouldn't take any shit from male drivers, either.

Barry shook his head free of memories and musings and went back to work.

Odd, though, that no one answered the telephone.

2

Barry finished the first stack of reports before he thought he would. He stood up, stretching until his muscles protested and his joints popped, then turned out the desk lamp and got ready to close up.

He'd tried three more times to call his dad in New Orleans. Never gotten anyone to answer. And that was beginning to worry him.

He flipped the desk lamp back on and picked up an address book. Crap! He'd never get to sleep unless he found out *something* about his dad. He looked up the home number of Jim Carson, a man who'd been with Big Joe for over twenty years, and punched out the number.

His wife, Ginny, answered the phone.

"Barry!" she said, her affection for him evident over the distance. "It's so good to hear from you. You still baching it?"

"Oh, yeah. Ginny, is Jim there?"

"No. He just called from Memphis. He picked up a load there; taking it to Chicago."

"Ginny, I'm trying to get in touch with Dad. I called the plant, but couldn't get an answer."

"Well . . ." she hesitated.

"Come on, Ginny. What's wrong down there?"

"Big Joe had to cut back on personnel, Barry. It's just the bad times; you know. The terminal is dark at night."

Barry didn't believe that for a second. Rivers Trucking had been in the good black on anybody's books for years. But let Ginny play it her way.

"So where's Dad?"

"Barry, now don't get excited; it's nothing serious. But he's in the hospital."

"The *hospital?*"

"Barry, calm down. Joe will be back home tomorrow. I'm going to pick him up personally. He just had . . . an accident, that's all."

That's all? "What kind of accident, Ginny?"

"Wrench slipped. Broke, I think. Busted some ribs."

Should I tell her I'm coming down? No, he made up his mind. No, and I won't tell Pop, either. 'Cause Ginny is holding back from me. Or flat-out lying. "OK, Ginny. I'll call him at home tomorrow. You'll tell him?"

"Sure, Barry. You take care now."

She hung up.

Strange, Barry thought, replacing the receiver. Something is wrong down there. Very wrong.

He checked the offices and small kitchen/lounge, turning out the lights, slipped into his sport coat, and set the alarm system. He stepped out into the coolness of early spring and walked to the parking area of Rivers Consulting. He was deep in thought and not expecting trouble. It jarred him when two men stepped out of the darkness, one facing him, the other behind him.

"No trouble, now, buddy," the man facing him said. "Just hand over your money and watch and money clip. You rich bastards carry them, I know."

It took Barry about two seconds to get over his surprise. Then he got mad as hell.

Barry Rivers had worked hard all his life. He had no patience with those who chose the so-called "easy way." And Barry was no cherry when it came to hand-to-hand fighting. He'd grown up rough-and-tumble, around wildcat drivers; he had worked the oil fields, both actively and hauling equipment to them.

And he hated punks. He knew the definition of that word had changed over the years, at least in certain quarters, but to him a punk was still a punk: a low-down, worthless, thieving son of a bitch.

He had no way of knowing whether the men were armed. He could see no weapons; neither man was carrying a visible knife or gun. His Cajun temper boiled to the surface, then his hard training took precedence, softening his sudden rage, chilling him, honing him back into what Uncle Sammy had made him: a killing machine.

He suddenly whirled, his right foot kicking up as high as a ballet dancer's, the side of his shoe catching the man who had faced him on the side of his jaw. The man stumbled backward, blood leaking from the side of his mouth. Barry completed his full-circle whirl and came face to face with the other man, crouching, his hands open, moving in the classic unarmed combat stance.

"Hey, man!" the punk said just before Barry popped him on the side of the face with his left hand and broke his collarbone with the knife edge of his right hand.

The would-be mugger screamed in pain as his right arm dangled, useless.

Whirling, Barry kicked the first punk in the balls, doubling him over, puking, on the asphalt. Barry then calmly, and with much malice aforethought, deliberately kicked the punk in the face, just as hard as he could. Without turning around, smelling the other craphead close behind him, Barry drove his elbow into the guy's stomach, just at the junction of the ribcage spread. The air whooshed out of the punk and Barry turned, bringing his balled fist down on the back of the man's neck. The man dropped to the parking lot. His neck looked like it was broken.

The old Fats Domino song came to Barry's mind: "Ain't That A Shame?"

Barry straightened and looked around him. No witnesses. Good. The dimly lit parking area was void of human life, not counting the shitheads on the asphalt. And Barry didn't count them as human.

He had no intention of calling the police. He knew that very little, or nothing, would come of that, except he'd be tied up in court, watching some asshole judge turn the men loose. And then Barry would probably be sued by the very crapheads who'd tried to mug him. For violating their constitutional rights, of course.

One of the punks moaned. Barry kicked him in the head, dropping him back into unconsciousness. As he did, a gun slipped from the man's belt, clattering on the asphalt.

"Cute," Barry muttered. He picked the gun up and stuck it in his jacket pocket. Looked like a nice .380 automatic.

He waited until a car passed by, then dragged the men to the alley behind his office and stuffed them into a dumpster, none too gently. He patted each of them on the head and walked away, toward his car. He had worked up an appetite.

Barry went to his apartment and fixed a salad and sandwich and a large glass of milk, taking the tray into the spacious den. He kicked off his shoes and sat down in a lounger. He tried the TV while he was eating, but there was nothing on the tube that seemed to hold his interest.

He finished his late meal, rinsed the dishes and stuck them in the dishwasher, along with the other dirty dishes. A typical bachelor, Barry detested washing dishes. When the dishwasher got full, he turned it on. A maid came in once a week to handle the other housekeeping chores.

He showered and hit the sack. He slept better than he had in months, due in no small part to the fact that he turned off the phone before he went to bed.

The police were waiting at his office when he arrived the next morning.

They weren't totally unexpected. Barry had felt that when the would-be muggers were discovered—if they were discovered before they could wander off—the cops would run a check on who owned the building and who leased the offices.

The county cops knew who Barry was and what he did for a living. And this wasn't the first time he had hammered on thieves.

The first time, when he had just moved to his present location, Barry had played it the straight and legal way—calling the police, making his statement, going to the police station, enduring all the annoying bullshit. Finally his case had come to court. The judge gave the crapheads three years' probation. They turned around and sued Barry. They moaned and whined and sobbed and told the jury how the big bad ol' man had beat them up, breaking some of their bones in the process. It just hadn't been necessary to use all that force, man. All they'd been doing, they explained to the jury, was breaking into the guy's office, trashing it, tearing up some old stuff, and stealin' some other stuff.

Barry settled out of court for five thousand bucks apiece. It cost him weeks of lost work, thousands of dollars in legal fees, untold aggravation, plus the settlement.

"Gentlemen," Barry greeted the cops. "Something I can do for you?"

"Perhaps," the older of the cops said, his streetwise eyes inspecting Barry. "Two young men were found in the dumpster behind this office complex last night. They had been badly beaten. They're both at the hospital."

"At taxpayer's expense, I'm sure," Barry said dryly. The cop had not said "in" the hospital, but "at."

The cop's eyes narrowed at that crack.

But this time Barry had done his best to foil any legal work on behalf of the street-slime. He had carefully washed his shoes after going to his apartment. He had then spit-shined them, in high-gloss military fashion. He had dumped his shirt, underwear, and socks into the washer, then into the dryer, and folded and put them away. He had dropped off his car at a service station, after vacuuming it out that morning, to have it washed and vacuumed again. He had field-stripped the .380 and dropped the parts off at various trash cans.

Now let the cops do their best with what they had to work with.

Barry had no beef with the cops—they had a job to do and had to do it—it was the legal system that annoyed him.

"Would you know anything about the young men, Mr. Rivers?" the cop asked.

"I know I didn't give you my name."

"We checked."

"I'm sure you did. No. I don't know a thing about the young men."

"Did you work late here last night, sir?"

"I certainly did. I worked until about nine-thirty or ten, then locked up and went home."

"And you didn't hear any sounds of a struggle or a fight while you were here?"

"Not a peep."

"See anyone hanging around when you left the building?"

"No one."

"Of course you would have notified the police had you seen anyone suspicious?"

"Oh, of course, officer."

The cop smiled at him. Turning to his younger partner, he said, "Make one more sweep of the alley, Jimmy. Take your time." His partner gone, the cop looked at Barry. "Don't bullshit me, Mr. Rivers. You were Seventh Special Forces, I was Tenth Special Forces. I did a little checking on you, early this morning. You got burned by some crapheads some years back. Now you know our legal system has some holes in it, but it's still the system we have to live by and with. You've hammered on punks before, Mr. Rivers. Since that time you got burned. Outside that supper club not too far from here was one. The second was that time at the airport parking area. Probably more, but those come to mind. Oh, we can't prove it, so relax. It's just that you were in the area those nights, and you're hoss enough, with the right temperament to do it. OK. Fine with me,

Mr. Rivers. I share your opinion of thieves. Just don't bull-shit me, Colonel.''

Barry smiled at the man and the man returned the smile. "What do you want me to say?" Barry asked.

"Nothing. It's over. The punk with the busted face won't talk, and the one with the broken neck died about five hours ago."

Barry did not change expression. Like the man had said, "at the hospital."

The cop grunted. "You're a cold one, Colonel. I'd sure hate to make you mad at me."

"Have a nice day, officer."

3

"What in the world was that all about, Barry?" Maggie asked.

Barry told her, while his other coworkers, and his partner in the firm, Jack Morris, gathered around and listened.

When Barry finished, Jack shook his head in disgust and said, "This damn place is getting worse, not better."

Barry laughed and patted his chubby partner on the back. "Signs of the times, Jack." He motioned his partner into his office and waved him to a seat.

"Anything serious?" Jack asked. Jack was a constant worrier; he just wasn't happy unless he had something to fret about.

"Nothing at all, Jack. I'm going to take a vacation, that's all."

"Oh. Well . . . good! You had me worried. Hell, Barry. You're certainly due a vacation. You haven't had one in . . . what? Two-three years?"

"Something like that. I don't know how long I'm going to be gone this time."

That worried look again. Now Jack seemed more natural. "The specs we're working on for the Pentagon?"

"I'm getting on them today. If I can finish them, I'll pull out on Saturday. If not, whenever I finish, I'll leave. I'm going to take several weeks, Jack; maybe a month. But I'm not going to leave anything hanging. Maggie can run this part, and I'll keep in touch."

Jack rose with a grunt and a smile. "Then, I guess we'd all better get cracking."

The remainder of the week passed by in a blur of work. Barry called his father, who assured him everything was just fine. Just a stupid accident.

But Barry knew his dad too well. His dad was worried about something, and it was something he wasn't going to let his son in on.

Barry had one brother, one sister. His younger brother, Paul, was an attorney in Baton Rouge. His sister, Donna, the baby of the family, was married, and lived in Houston. Barry and Paul had never been close. Paul was studious and very reserved and had never approved of Barry's life-style. And Barry had never approved of his brother's chosen profession. Paul was forever running off to defend some damned punk; moaning and pissing about the poor unfortunate criminals. Barry hadn't seen him or talked with him in five years.

Donna had finished school at LSU and then taught school for several years before marrying an attorney. Another damned lawyer in the family. But Barry did communicate with his sister. He didn't like her husband, but he loved his baby sister.

There was no serious woman in Barry's life. After Julie, he had become gun-shy when it came to getting close—emotionally—with any lady. He kept company with half a dozen career women in and around the D.C. area. Including one lady lawyer with the Justice Department.

He reached for the phone and called Linda. "How about a working lunch today?"

"Oh, my," she said. "Anytime the elusive Colonel Rivers calls, I get used. What's the deal, Barry?"

"Tell you over lunch."

"Can you make it over here in thirty minutes?"

"I will do my best, Miss O'Day."

"Ms.," she corrected.

"Right."

Neither one of them was a heavy drinker, so they each ordered a glass of white wine and talked while waiting for lunch.

"I know, Linda, from what you've told me in the past, that you're working on mob influence in New Orleans."

Her face remained impassive.

"I'm not asking for any confidential information. It's just that I have a sneaking suspicion someone is putting the pressure on my father. If Dad's in trouble, I'd like to know about it."

She looked at him for a moment. "Barry, I'm sorry. But I just didn't put the two together. Does your father own Rivers Trucking?"

"Yes."

She shook her head. "Incredible. What a small world it really is. I mean, you just never talked much about your family."

"I understand. Is the mob squeezing my father, Linda?"

"Well, you didn't get this from me, Barry. OK?" She seemed a bit eager to Barry. That was odd.

"You know it is."

"It looks like it. I'll have to go back and review the file, but Rivers Trucking is certainly one that we're investigating."

"You don't think my father . . ."

"Oh, God, no! It's just that the local capo of New Orleans, a toad by the name of Fabrello, wants to sew up New Orleans. And of course, we've known for a long time that the mob is heavily into certain aspects of the trucking industry."

"I'm going to take a leave of absence from the firm, Linda. I'll be going to New Orleans." He watched her face light up. "Something on your mind, Ms. O'Day?"

"Quite possibly, Colonel Rivers."

"Uh-huh. Now comes the payback, right?"

"Could be, buddy. You owe me several favors, remember?"

"Oh, yes."

"It's nothing great. You just report back to me anything you find suspicious. And don't be a hero, Barry. The war's over, even if you warrior types don't like the outcome."

"The war will never be over as long as there is the rumor of just one American being held P.O.W. in that goddamned hellhole."

She smiled at him. "It's coming back to me now, Barry. During our . . ." She blushed. Honest to God blushed. ". . . quiet times."

After the screwing, Barry thought. Being a tactful person he didn't say it aloud.

"And I know what you're thinking, you heathen, and you'd better not say it."

" 'Nary a crude word will pass my lips, dear."

"Right. How about it, Barry—a deal?"

"With a condition, yes."

"What condition?"

"A federal permit to carry a gun."

"Barry, I just told you, no heroics."

"That's the condition."

"I have a friend with Treasury. I might get you sworn in as some type of special agent. I don't know if there *is* such a thing as a federal permit to carry a gun."

"Well, find out. See if your friend can get me sworn in as an agent."

She called him that evening.

"Barry? It's iffy. And it doesn't look good."

"I go armed, Linda. Either way. If I'm sticking my hand in a snake pit for Uncle Sammy, the least Uncle could do is arm me."

"Well . . . let me work on it."

"OK. Call me at the office tomorrow."

Barry was determined to make it by Friday evening. He had put in twelve- and fifteen-hour days to do it, but he was going to get clear of the city Saturday afternoon, at the latest. He began packing. Early spring in New Orleans can be tricky, weatherwise. Might be eighty-five degrees one day and fifty-five the next, so he packed for spring and summer.

And Linda still had not called. He had tried calling her at work, but she was always busy. He got the feeling he was getting the runaround, which wasn't like her at all.

She finally called him Friday morning at work.

"I tell you what, buddy. I had to pull every string I knew of and then some. But you'll get your federal permit. Can you meet me at Treasury at noon?"

"Sure. I'm caught up."

"Might take two or three hours, Barry."

"To sign my name a couple of times?"

She laughed. Not too pleasantly, Barry felt. "It might entail a bit more than that, Colonel. See you," she said cheerfully, then hung up.

"This form," the man said, "absolves us of any responsibility should you get hurt, Colonel Rivers. This form states that you waived any medical coverage or life insurance."

The man droned on and on. Barry signed his name at least fifty times, or so it seemed to him. He was fingerprinted and mugged and sworn in. Then he was given an ID card, sealed in plastic, with his picture and thumbprint. Very impressive-looking card. *UNITED STATES TREASURY DEPARTMENT—BUREAU OF ALCOHOL, TOBACCO, AND FIREARMS.*

Barry had dealt with the government for many, many years. He had worked for and with the CIA, DIA, and a dozen other spook agencies.

And he didn't trust a goddamned one of them. He'd had too many mercenary friends who'd been left high and dry and tortured to death in foreign countries after the agency they were working for disowned them and let them die.

Barry had tape-recorded the day's entire procedure, using a tape recorder no bigger than a matchbox. He'd been certain to repeat each person's name—and what he was to do next and what to sign—at least twice. His attorney was waiting for him outside the building.

"Who the hell is this?" Linda demanded, eyeballing the man suspiciously.

"My attorney, Linda. Ralph Martin." He handed the

attorney the tiny recorder, tape still inside. "Mr. Martin specializes in kicking the shit out of punks in court; after the courts have kicked the shit out of his clients."

"Doesn't he have a marvelous way with words, Ms. O'Day?" Ralph said, grinning. He handed the recorder to another man. "So nice to meet you, Ms. O'Day."

"Who is that other man!" Linda said.

"That, Linda," Barry said, "is a fellow from a group called IOLDG. Intelligence Officers' Legal Defense Group. I think you've heard of them."

"Barry," Linda said, her voice very nervous. "This is bullshit. This wasn't part of the deal."

"I'll just run along," the IOLDG man said. "I'll have copies of this tape made and transcribed to paper. Sign them before you leave, Barry."

Barry nodded. "See you, Walt."

"Barry . . ." Linda said, a definite warning in her voice.

"It's the old Army game, Linda," he said. "CYA. Cover Your Ass."

Linda flushed. "I've a mind to go back in there and have them pull that card, Barry."

"Oh, that wouldn't look very good, Ms. O'Day," Ralph said. "The press would just love to get something like this to squawk about, don't you agree?"

Linda whirled on Barry. "You . . . *prick!*" she shouted.

An elderly lady, a tourist by the looks of her, stopped and stared at Linda. "See," she said to her equally elderly companion. "I told you that's where the ERA would lead."

They marched on.

"Let me see your ID card, Barry," Ralph said, holding out his hand.

Barry gave it to him.

"Good. No expiration date. Treasury's got you for as long as you want them to."

Linda was turning about seven different shades. And both Barry and Ralph knew that Treasury would be pissing on themselves when they found out what had gone down. And they would find out, just as soon as Linda could get to them.

"Care to have dinner at my place this evening?" Barry asked Linda.

She started to tell him to take his dinner invitation and shove it, but the humor of the situation finally hit home. She began smiling. "Yeah," she said. "I'll take you up on that, Colonel. And it better be a good dinner, 'cause you damn sure owe me one. I'm going to get in all sorts of trouble over this little deal."

"They'll get over it. 'Bout seven all right?"

"I'll be there. With a brief case full of information . . . Agent Rivers."

4

Barry got away at noon Saturday, driving his pickup truck. His suitcases and garment bag were in the back, covered with a tarp and tied down. Inside the toolbox, which was bolted to the bed of the truck, in a false bottom, lying on foam-rubber padding, locked in place by rubber-coated brackets, was Barry's New Orleans insurance . . . in case things turned rough in the Crescent City.

Two nickel-plated S&W Model 39 9mm semiautomatic pistols. One Uzi submachine gun. One Ruger Mini-14. Spare clips for each weapon, and forty boxes of ammo. He had leather for the pistols and a little plastic-enclosed card in his pocket that said it was all legal.

He still chuckled over that deal.

Treasury had squawked and squalled and moaned and finally settled down, grim-faced, with more than one member of Treasury hiding a smile, seeing the humor in being set up and had by a civilian. The older, more experienced agents of BATF silently welcomed Barry aboard; they knew the colonel's reputation. They knew he would not flaunt his credentials; knew he would play it close to the vest, using his ID only if he got in a hard, tight spot with the local law. And they knew Colonel Barry Rivers was one randy son of a bitch who had about as much compassion toward punks and assholes and street-slime as a mongoose has for a cobra.

Zero.

Barry had stopped by the small offices of the IOLDG and signed the papers, sealing, only slightly illegally, the unwilling contract.

Linda had brought a briefcase full of papers to his apartment. He had committed as much of them as possible to memory. Names with faces, businesses with faces, mob enforcers, runners, whores, pimps, pushers, bag men and women . . . all connected with the local mob.

The dinner had been very good, and dessert was even better; took two to consummate it.

He spent the first night in a small motel in Virginia, the second in Alabama. It was there Barry unpacked his shoulder holster and dug out one of his 9mms. He loaded the clip and readied the weapon. He checked his little .25 caliber automatic. He carried that in an ankle holster, right side of his boot, inside. Inside his left boot, he carried a double-edged commando knife, honed razor sharp. The knife was good for one thing only: to kill.

Barry began psyching himself, bringing himself up, or down, depending on one's point of view, mentally. He had no illusions about New Orleans; about what he was stepping into. He was New Orleans born and reared, and he knew the mob. He had heard the name Fabrello all his life and he had seen, personally and up-close, what mob enforcers could do. He had seen people pulled from the river, from Lake Pontchartrain, Lake Salvador, and Lake Maurepas. He had seen the torture inflicted on those who elected to buck the mob.

No, he had no illusions.

But if the local strong-arm boys were muscling in on his dad, if they had hurt his dad . . . someone was going to pay. In blood.

And that was something the mob understood.

He pulled into a truck stop on Interstate 10, just outside Biloxi, when he spotted a Kenworth pulling a flatbed, parked on the asphalt. On the side of the door: *RIVERS TRUCKING*.

He parked his pickup in the passenger-car area and stepped out. It might be early spring, but it was just plain cold. He thought about slipping on his shoulder holster, then decided against it. It was too soon for that.

He walked into the cafe, his cowboy hat pulled low. His eyes found the familiar blue jacket of Rivers Trucking. He walked on past the man, sitting down in the booth behind the driver. He knew the driver's face, but could not recall his name. Just as well. Barry wanted several days of anonymity.

He ordered coffee and a club sandwich and waited. He knew it wouldn't be long before somebody would come in and know the driver, start up a conversation. That happened before the waitress even brought his coffee.

A Roadway driver came in and slid into the booth, facing the Rivers man. "Chuck," he said. "Thought you was hangin' it up with Rivers?"

"Last run, Lobo," Chuck said, using the driver's CB handle. "Me and Snake both turnin' in our time."

"Then the rumors is true?"

"I'm like them three monkeys, Lobo. I ain't seen nothin', heard nothin', and I ain't sayin' nothin'."

Snake would be that long lean drink of water from up in north Louisiana, Hal Grethal. CB handle, Snake. Barry remembered him. He'd been with Joe Rivers for many years. A top-notch driver with a perfect safety record. Things had to be bad if Snake was pulling out.

Barry waited.

"I know what you mean," Lobo said. "Like the time I was pullin' out of New Jersey for the Bertolli Brothers. Old Man Bertolli wouldn't let the local boys shake him down. Man, they put him out of business. I left before it got really rough. But I heard more than I wanted to hear . . ."

Barry didn't catch the rest of Lobo's statement. The waitress brought his sandwich and wanted to talk. Barry smiled at her and exchanged a few words. She returned his smile and left.

Leaving a silent invitation behind her with a faint scent of perfume.

". . . isn't just them folks," Chuck said. "Them . . . folks hired themselves a bunch of wildcat drivers. They can drive a truck, that's about the only good thing any decent driver could say about them. They're thugs and hoods and punks. It was them that ran ol' Billy Bob off the road out on Twenty, just east of Pecos. Crippled him up bad. He'll never drive again. And they got hoods in four-wheelers, shootin' at Rivers Trucks. I ain't tellin' you nothing you ain't already heard on the CB, Lobo."

"Yeah, it's all up and down the road."

And my CB quit working, Barry thought. Well, this truck stop has them. I'll buy a new one.

"Where you goin', Chuck?"

"I don't know. Snake's a little wishy-washy about leaving Big Joe. But Snake ain't married. I am. I got two kids in college, and I don't know what the old lady would do if something happened to me. Know what I mean?"

"Yeah."

The two drivers talked for a while longer, but nothing more about Big Joe's problems. They had a second cup of coffee and left, one heading west, the other east.

Barry left a tip and paid his check, then wandered into the gift shop. He bought a Midland forty-channel CB and went outside, pulling his truck around to the rear of the huge truck stop. It took him less than five minutes to pull out his old CB and remount the new one in the same brackets.

"You gonna test that thing out, citizen?" a female voice spoke from behind him.

Barry turned and looked into the face of an angel.

"Uh . . . yeah. Soon as I get on the road."

"Which way you headin'?" She was maybe five three. Blond. Natural blond—as far as Barry could tell. A traffic-stopping figure. Cowboy shirt, blue jeans, and boots. Blue eyes.

"West, into New Orleans."

"Yeah? Me, too. You watch them motherfuckin' cops just this side of Slidell. They'll nail your ass to the wall."

An angel with a garbage can for a mouth. "Thanks."

"You ever drive a truck, boy?"

"Long time ago. Why, does it show?"

"Yeah, kind of, I guess. You lookin' for a job, maybe?"

"Could be. Who you drive for?"

"Big Joe Rivers."

Barry had to hide his smile. He'd make a bet this little waif-looking blonde watched her gutter-mouth around his dad. Big Joe could and did cuss like a sailor . . . but not around women. He was old-fashioned that way. And he wouldn't tolerate a woman using bad language.

"Yeah? I've heard some talk about Rivers Trucking. Maybe I'd prefer to eat less and go on living?"

She put both hands on shapely hips and hung a cussin' on Barry. "Goddamnchickenshityankeebastard!"

Barry laughed at her. "Whoa! I didn't say I wasn't interested. I'm just telling you what I heard, that's all."

"This dude givin' you trouble, Kate?" a man's voice came from behind Barry.

Barry cut his eyes. A burly driver carrying a wooden tire knocker in his right hand stood just behind him.

"Goddamn coward, is all!" Kate spat the words at Barry.

"Maybe he's just got good sense," a second man's voice spoke.

"What the hell you mean?" Kate flared.

"I heard it all. Just gettin' out of my bunk. This guy didn't say nothin' to you to deserve the cussin' you hung on him, Kate. You can't blame a man for wantin' to stay alive."

"Why don't you take that boot you're holdin' and shove it in your mouth?" Kate yelled at him. "And stay out of my business."

"Whoa!" Barry said, raising his voice to be heard above Kate. The independent driver was hopping around, trying to pull on his boot. The East Texas Motor Freight driver still had the tire knocker in his hand. "This thing is getting out of hand."

"Well, you just apologize to Kate and we'll forget it," the ETMF man said.

"Apologize?" Barry said. "For *what?*"

" 'Cause I said so, buddy."

Barry's Cajun temper was rapidly coming to the surface. "Partner," he spoke to the ETMF driver, "you better get off my back before I kick your ass so hard you gonna feel like you been riding that camel all day instead of your tractor." Barry pointed to the logo painted on the trailer of the ETMF man.

"He probably feels that way now," a third man spoke. "Considerin' that piece of junk he's drivin'. I drove something that raggedy-assed lookin' I'd be ashamed to call myself a trucker."

Truck drivers insult each other on the average of about ten thousand times a day—per state. The ETMF man just grinned. But his grin was directed toward the driver, not toward Barry.

"I think I'll just whup your ass, boy," he said to Barry.

"With or without your club, hotshot?"

The ETMF man tossed the knocker to the driver who had insulted him. "Hold that. And don't steal it, you hound-dog-lookin' thing."

He swung at Barry. But Barry had anticipated the punch and sidestepped. The driver lost his balance and fell down.

"Goddamn, boy!" Kate said. "Defendin' me is one thing, but you gotta stand up to do it."

"Give me time, Kate!"

"I ought to kick your face in," Barry said. "But I feel sorry for you. If I was takin' this fight seriously, you'd be dead by now."

"I think I'd believe him was I you," the independent driver said, finally getting his boot on.

"Stay out of this, you damn hog-hauler!" the ETMF man said, getting to his feet. He assumed the classic boxer's stance and shuffled toward Barry.

Barry kicked him on the kneecap and clubbed him on the side of the head as he was going down.

"Driver," Barry said. "I don't want to hurt you. I know you've got a load to deliver. Let's just call it off before you make me mad."

Several drivers stepped in and pulled the ETMF man to his feet. "That's it," one said. "It's over. You're gonna get hurt bad if you keep on."

"Put some ice on that knee," Barry said. "And don't let it stiffen up."

"You a wahoo, boy," the independent said to Barry. He grinned and held out his hand. "They call me Cottonmouth. What's your handle?"

"Dog," Barry said. Ever since he'd read a book about an Army Dog Team he'd adopted the handle of Dog.

He shook the man's hand.

"You two gonna kiss each other?" Kate said.

Barry looked at her. "Has anybody ever told you that you're a troublemaker, miss?"

"Has anybody ever told you to *get fucked?*" she screamed at him. She whirled and marched into the truck stop.

"Kate!" the independent yelled. She stopped and spun around. "Tell Big Joe I'll be in soon as I drop this load over to Beaumont. That is, if he still wants to hire me."

"He does. And bring hotshot there with you. That is, if he's got the balls to drive for a real outfit."

"You'd be surprised what I can drive, spitfire," Barry told her.

"You probably couldn't drive a fuckin' vacuum cleaner around a living room," she fired back at him. She marched on into the truck stop.

"Kate Sherman," Cottonmouth said. "Ain't she something?"

Barry just looked at him.

"Rods that Kenworth up and down the highway better than most men. She likes you, too, Dog."

"*Likes* me? What would she do if she didn't like me—shoot me?"

"Probably," Cottonmouth drawled.

5

Barry and Cottonmouth leaned against Cottonmouth's Peterbilt and chatted.

"You wanna buy a rig?" he asked Barry.

"No," Barry said with a laugh. "You gettin' tired of driving independent or the bank closing in on you?"

"Bank. I got 'er almost paid for and had to refinance. Then, boy, the bottom dropped out." He patted the truck's fender. " '81 model. Double-wide walk-in sleeper. 400 Cummins. New clutch. Jake Brake, 13-speed, 240 wheelbase. 'Bout 85 percent rubber. Forty-five thousand and it's yours, Dog." He grinned.

"She's pretty," Barry said. She was pulling a reefer. "But I guess not. That old boy with ETMF hold a grudge?"

"Naw. He just got his ass whipped, that's all. Everybody kinds of looks after Kate. But don't let her size fool you. She's stout, and she'll fight, too. And she's loyal to Big Joe Rivers. She got in trouble 'bout, oh, eight years ago, I reckon. Shot her old man when he was beatin' up on her. Big Joe knew her momma and came to Kate's defense. Taught her to drive personal. Kate never knew her daddy, so Joe became like one to her.''

"From what I hear, Cottonmouth, you might be stepping into a lot of trouble going to work for Rivers.''

"Yeah, maybe. But Joe starts drivers off at twenty cents a mile, good vacation and insurance, loadin' and unloadin' pay. I ain't makin' no money as an independent. I drove three hundred hours last month, and after my expenses, I figure I made less than three dollars an hour. That ain't no livin'. 'Sides,'' he said with a grin, ''I don't like to see no one like Joe Rivers bein' crowded out of business by a bunch of crud like the mob. You know what I mean?''

Barry knew. He liked this guy who called himself Cottonmouth. But he wasn't ready to fully trust him yet. ''I might drop by and see Joe Rivers. Maybe I'll see you around the terminal.''

"Could be, Dog. Could be. I gotta get me some breakfast. You eat yet?''

Typical long-distance hauler, Barry thought. It's afternoon and he wants breakfast. His days and nights are all turned around. ''Yeah. Good to meet you, Cottonmouth. Hope I run into you again.''

"You prob'ly will. Where'd you learn to fight like that, anyways?''

Barry smiled. ''Special Forces.''

Cottonmouth laughed. ''Wait 'till I tell ol' camel-humper that. He'll shit. See you 'round, Dog.''

It didn't come as any surprise to Barry when he looked in his mirrors and saw the big blue Kenworth sitting about three feet from his rear bumper. Barry smiled and reached for his mike.

"Go to twelve, Kate," he said. Channel twelve. Most of the trucker traffic is on channel nineteen.

He switched over and waited.

"All right. So I'm on twelve. What do you want, hotshot?" Kate's voice came through the speaker.

"What's your handle?"

"TNT." That figured.

"You over your mad yet?" he asked, knowing full well probably fifty people had switched over when he did and were listening. For most, it wasn't being nosy. Not really. Long-distance hauls are lonely. Anything to break the monotony.

"I might be. What's it to you?"

"Just curious."

"Dog suits you right well, boy," TNT said. "A yellow dog."

"Maybe you got me wrong, TNT. Try that on for size. You copy?"

"Yeah, I copy. Maybe so. You might be a trucker. But you something else, too. I ain't quite got your figured out yet. But I will."

"If you hate me so bad, why go to all that trouble?"
Silence.

"I wish you'd answer him," a man's voice said. "I hate a mystery."

" 'S'at you, Red?" Kate hollered.

"Yes'um."

"Get off this channel, you prick! This is a private conversation. You hear me?"

"Yes, *ma'am!*"

"I don't know, Dog. Something 'bout you that puzzles me. But I ain't fixin' to talk about it on the air—you copy?"

"Yeah. So if you don't mind, I'll get in the rocking chair, ten-four?"

"Come on."

Barry changed lanes, reduced speed, and pulled in behind her.

"Just stay with me, Dog. Go back to nineteen."

They rolled into Louisiana and Barry waited until Kate had weighed her load. On Interstate 10, just before crossing the Pontchartrain, Kate signaled she was pulling over. Barry pulled in behind her and got out.

They stood on the right side of Kate's rig, the Kenworth giving them some protection from the rush and wind of southbound traffic.

"You a movie star or something?" she demanded. "Out slummin', maybe?"

"No. Why do you ask?"

" 'Cause I've seen you somewheres. You damned familiar to me. TV newsman, maybe?"

"No. I own a business up in Maryland. I'm on vacation."

"Liar! Part of what you say is probably true. But something about you rings false. And that bothers me."

"Where do you live, Kate?"

She studied him with cautious blue eyes. They were so blue they almost hurt him to look at them. "Trailer park just west of the city." She gave him the address.

"Do you always give your address to strangers?"

"No," she said quickly. "But Cottonmouth says you're a hundred percent. I been knowin' that ol' boy for years. I trust him. 'Sides, I got a .38 stuck down in my boot and a twenty-gauge shotgun by the door of my trailer house. You know what I mean?"

Barry knew. He debated for a moment whether or not to level with her. He decided to wait awhile. "You got a phone?"

"I'm in the book. Cottonmouth said he told you my name."

"Yeah. There a motel near where you live?"

"Yeah. They're easy to find." Her eyes once more searched his face. "Let me put something on you, Dog. What the hell is your name, anyway?"

"Barry." He took a chance.

"Barry. All right. You may be the genuine article. I hope so. But if you're workin' for that frog-eyed son of a bitch Fabrello, you gonna be in deep shit."

They both looked up as a Peterbilt pulled off the interstate, hissing to a stop close to them. Cottonmouth's rig.

"See you, Barry," Kate said.

Cottonmouth climbed down and walked to Barry's side. He waited until Kate had pulled out, then said, "Don't get the wrong idea 'bout Kate, Dog. 'Cause if you're looking for an easy lay, you best keep on lookin'. You know where I'm comin' from?"

"Yeah, I know. I got the impression she cusses as a protective measure, and nothing more."

"Uh-huh. So you got some education, too. Lemme put something else on you, Dog. You try to mess up Kate, and you'll never get out of Louisiana alive."

"Yeah? I figured that out, too."

"See you 'round."

Barry checked into a small motel not far from Kate's address, then drove to his dad's teminal. Ten Kenworths were parked next to the fence. From the dust covering them, they had not been used in a long time. Several months, at least. The terminal area was clean, but deserted. Kate's blue Kenworth was backed up to the loading dock. The way she'd been rolling, Barry had figured she was deadheading back from somewhere. There was a time, not too long ago, when no Rivers truck ever deadheaded back from anywhere.

So business was that far off.

Barry did not want to draw attention to himself, so he slipped his truck into gear and eased out. He drove past a cream-colored sedan parked not far from the business. There was no mistaking the two men sitting in the front seat. They both had the mark of punks about them, despite the expensive sports coats they wore. And they were staring at Barry through hard eyes.

Barry checked his mirrors. The street behind him was deserted. He swung his eyes to the men in the sedan. They were still staring at him. He braked and returned the stares.

Impasse in the middle of the street.

"I fascinate you boys?" Barry asked.

"Carry your ass, cowboy," the driver said.

"Fuck you!" Barry said, his eyes unblinking and hard.

The punk on the passsenger side got out. He was big and solid and looked to be about six three, at least; maybe two hundred and thirty pounds. But he had the beginnings of a beer belly. He walked around Barry's pickup, noting the license plates.

"In case you can't read," Barry said. "The number is five–eight–seven–one–one–four." It wasn't that at all.

"You about a smartass, ain't you?" Beer Belly said. "Wait a minute, that ain't the number!" He started back around the truck. Confused, as Barry had hoped he would be, after calling out the wrong numbers.

Barry jerked the pickup into reverse and backed up, almost hitting the guy, putting the license plate out of his view.

"You asshole!" Beer Belly said. "I think you need your jaw jacked."

Beer Belly walked up to the driver's side, his hands clenched into big fists. Barry opened the door—hard, knocking the man sprawling to the dirty street. Barry stepped out of the truck just as Beer Belly was getting to his hands and knees. Barry kicked him in the face with his right cowboy boot. Teeth rolled and bounced on the street, glistening wet and white, red-stained.

The driver was getting out. Barry leaped and hit the door, slamming it against the driver. The edge of the door caught the man in his belly. He screamed in pain and doubled over just in time to catch Barry's boot in his mouth. He was out before his head hit the street.

Barry looked around him. No traffic. He opened the trunk and stuffed Beer Belly in the cavity, slamming the lid shut. He stuffed the driver into the back seat and took the keys out of the ignition, tossing them into a garbage can. He got into his pickup and drove off.

Across the street, standing on the loading dock, Jim Carson smiled and said, "Well, I'll just be damned. The boy's come home."

Kate stood beside him, her mouth still open in shock at seeing a much smaller man whip the hell out of two bigger men.

"What do you mean, Jim?" she asked. "You know that cowboy?"

"Know him? Hell, yes, I know him. That's Big Joe's boy. Barry. Ex-Green Beret; Medal of Honor winner. Now, Kate, my girl, things are looking up for Rivers Trucking."

Kate looked at the deserted street. "I just knew there was *something* about him I cottoned to."

6

"You really think you're something, don't you?" Kate challenged Barry, talking before she got the door to her trailer open.

She had bathed and washed her corn-yellow hair, tying it back with a red bandanna. She wore just a touch of perfume, but it was wrong for her, Barry noted; too heavy. But he wasn't about to object; not with Kate's temper. She had dressed in designer jeans and blouse. She looked delicious.

"What do you mean, Kate?"

"All that bull you spouted. All the time you being Big Joe's son. Well, hell! Don't just stand there. Come on in."

Barry entered the trailer and it was as he'd thought it would be: neat and clean. "You didn't ask me my last name, remember?"

"Uh-huh. Big Joe know you're here?"

"How did you discover who I was?"

"Sit down. Don't stand around lookin' like a lost hound dog." Barry sat. "Me and Jim Carson was watching the fight out front of the terminal. He told me. You know who them boys was, don't you?"

"No. But I can guess. Fabrello's men, probably, right?"

"Right. And *nobody* messes with Fabrello's men. You gonna be in trouble, boy. They find out where you stayin', somebody's liable to wire a bomb under the hood of your pickup."

"Maybe." Anybody who lifted the hood of Barry's truck without flipping a hidden switch under the dash was going to be in for a very loud and rude surprise. "But maybe I took some of the heat off Dad and you drivers. Think about that."

She plopped down in a chair and stared at him. "Maybe. But why would you set yourself up for us? I can see why you'd do it for Big Joe, but why do it for people you don't even know?"

"I hate punks," he said simply. And he did, passionately. He had lost two close friends to street-shit. One in D.C., one in New York City. His friend in D.C. had been mugged and killed; the killing had apparently been done for perverse pleasure, for Barry's friend had lost both legs to a mine in 'Nam. His friend in NYC had gotten caught in a crossfire between rival NYC mobs.

Kate shivered.

"You cold?"

"No. Your words caused a shiver to go up and down my back. I think you're a dangerous man, Barry Rivers."

"If that's true, than there are a lot of us walking around."

"Yeah," she agreed. "But mostly you guys cool it, I think. You hungry?"

"I could eat."

"Then, come on. You're takin' me to dinner."

* * *

The restaurant she guided him to was small and family-owned, and the smell of redfish cooking made Barry realize how much he'd missed New Orleans and her food. The owner and his wife greeted Kate as one might greet a long-absent daughter. Barry could tell they were more than fond of her. The couple gave Barry a good once-over and then spoke to Kate in rapid-fire Cajun French. Barry let them finish and then informed them he had spoken Cajun before he spoke English.

The man and woman smiled, then laughed as they guided Barry and Kate to a table. They ordered, then Barry said, "In answer to a question of yours, Kate. I imagine Dad knows I'm here by now. Jim probably told him. How is Dad?"

"Not too good. Fabrello's men leaned on him pretty good. Busted some ribs and broke an arm."

Barry fought back a sudden surge of temper. "At Dad's age, that's a tough lick."

"He'll never regain full use of his arm," Kate said quietly, but with considerable heat in her voice.

"We'll eat and then we'll go see him. That OK with you?"

"I'd like that."

Big Joe Rivers sat down in his chair and cried. Barry had never seen his father cry before. He didn't know what to do. And he had never seen his father looking like this. The man appeared to have aged twenty years since Barry had last seen him. He looked . . . like an old man.

Defeated.

Barry left Kate and his father and went into the kitchen,

pouring three glasses of wine, stalling, giving his dad time to pull himself together. And giving himself time to get his emotions back under control.

Defeated!

That word hit Barry hard. Suddenly, he knew what his dad was going to do.

No! What his dad was going to *try* to do.

But Barry wasn't going to allow that. Big Joe Rivers was not defeated, not finished, not through. Not by a long shot. Barry was going to prop his dad back up. By force, if he had to; even if his father was unwilling, which would probably be the case.

Barry took the wine into the den and sat down in front of his dad. "You look like shit, old man," he said bluntly.

Kate's look was one of utter disbelief and astonishment. She opened her mouth to speak, then closed it. She was an outsider, to a degree; this was father-and-son business.

A spark from a fading ember shot through the eyes of Joe Rivers. "You don't talk to me like that, you pup! I'll box your smart mouth."

"You couldn't box anybody's mouth, old man. Why don't you just sit there and give up?"

"What I do with my business is my business, you smart-mouth! Who axed you to come down here, get *fouiner*, anyways?"

"Nobody. You want me to leave?"

"Non. You can *roder autour de.* Just stay out of my affairs."

"My affairs, too, you old goat. Are you forgetting part of the business is mine?"

"So I'll write you out, you get too smart."

"That's your ass, too. I'll get the courts to declare you to be *fou!* I'll put you away where a *folle* belongs."

Big Joe glared at his son. "Now you listen to me, boy.

I'm not going to endanger any more of my drivers. I'm selling out. And that's final."

"You can't sell out, Papa. Not without the permission of the kids. Now Paul might give you his permission; he's such a wimp. But I won't, and Donna won't. Not when she hears the whole story. Now you just drink your wine and think about that for a minute."

Father and son glared at each other. Kate sat quietly in her chair, knowing now what Barry was doing. She had not told Barry that she thought his dad felt himself whipped. Beaten. Maybe Barry could bring this off. She wasn't sure.

Big Joe slumped back in his chair. "So what do you want to do, boy?"

"You retain your controlling interest in Rivers Trucking, Dad. But you name me, put on paper, make it legal, as chairman of the board and CEO."

"I don't know from nothing about no damned CEO. What's that mean?"

"Chief executive officer. In other words, I make all the decisions and no one can overrule me."

"So? *Alors qui?*"

"Then you take a vacation, Pop. Get clear and keep your head down. I'll take care of it."

"Boy, you know who you'd be up against? Teddy Fabrello. Old Frog Face. You wanna commit suicide, go do it somewheres else. I won't have your death on my hands."

"It's worth a try, Big Joe," Kate said.

Joe looked at her, his eyes softening. He loved the woman like a daughter. "Hey, *ma petite*. You a good driver. I give you a rig. Everything. Sign it over to you. Clear. Don't listen to this crazy son of mine. He get you killed, girl."

Kate slumped back, her blue eyes blazing. "I never thought Big Joe Rivers would turn chicken."

"Would you listen to this little chickie chirp?" Joe said, looking at Barry. "Five feet two inches tall and she's going to fight the mob. You know what they do to pretty little things like you, girl? Nasty things. *Sale!* Lemme tell you both something about what is happening here. It ain't all what it seems. Fabrello is bein' used by somebody. Fabrello don't give a sack of shrimp for my little trucking operation. The mob is being used—but they don't know it."

Barry leaned back in his chair. Big Joe's face had toughened and so had his voice. He was showing some of the fire that Barry remembered. "What are you talking about, Dad?"

Joe Rivers was thoughtful for a few seconds. "OK. OK. Kate, Barry, what you hear now, what I'm about to say, it don't leave this room. You, Kate, it'll get you killed, girl. I mean it. *Comprendre?*"

"*Oui.*"

"OK. *Tout de bon.* Some big shots from Washington, they flew down to see me. *Me!* Joe Rivers. I come out with a contract worth millions of dollars. Whole operation is gonna change. Pretty soon, we gonna be pulling SSTs. FBI, they come in and check everybody out. Reason I fire Benny? Bad record in his past. Stealin'. I didn't know that about him. Well, too bad for Benny." He shrugged philosophically. "Now, it stands to reason that nobody with no mob contacts could get a contract pullin' SSTs—right? You both know that. So the way I figure it, the reason the local press ain't jumped all over this thing is that Fabrello didn't report back to New York. He bein' paid privately to put pressure on me, the money coming from outside the mob. But I don't know where."

SSTs. Safe Secure Transports. A government term for

trailers that haul top-secret military equipment. Warheads, chemicals, prototypes. Two drivers to a rig; both heavily armed. Both well trained.

Barry looked at Kate. Back to his dad. "Now, wait a minute! . . ."

Big Joe smiled. "Yeah, boy. It don't figure, does it?"

"What else, Dad?"

"Well, when old Frog Face and his boys start puttin' the lean on me, I call this special number the FBI men gave me. They say, 'Oh, we sorry, Mr. Rivers. We'll take care of the matter right away. But don't call no other number but this one.' OK, I say. Fine. But the pressure don't stop. It don't make no sense, boy. I know the mob ain't got the FBI in their pocket."

"Give me the number, Pop."

Barry took the number and walked to the phone. It was a Washington area number, but it was the wrong area code for the main FBI office in D.C. He looked back at his dad. "How many times have you called this number, Dad?"

"Two times."

"Same person answer the phone both times?"

"Ahhh . . . no."

He put his hand on the phone, then pulled it back. "Where'd you make the calls, Dad?"

"One from the office, one from here. Just like they told me to do."

"Why would they tell you to do that?"

" 'Cause they said they'd checked these phones and they was secure. Made sense to me—then."

"What they are is bugged."

"Yeah, I figured that out, too."

Barry thought the house might be wired for sound, too. But if so, they'd already said too much. Hell with it. He walked to the stereo and turned it to radio, tuning into a

Cajun station, turning the volume up. "I'm going to check this number out, Dad. But not from here. Something isn't jelling about this whole operation. It's almost as if the mob influence is secondary."

"Uh-huh."

"But why?"

"I don't know. But I been thinkin' about it some. Look here." He pulled out a trucker's atlas. "First load comes out of Fort Huachuca, Arizona. That's hauled to a site in Nevada. Next load comes out of Yuma Proving Grounds in Nevada. That's hauled up to north California. Third load is hauled out of Texas. Fort Bliss. You wanna tie those three places together, boy?"

At first, Barry didn't get it. Then it came to him. All three places were central to Mexico. "All right," he said. "Mexico."

"Go on," Joe Rivers urged.

Barry shrugged. Then the dim light in his head brightened. "Dope."

"Cocaine. That's all I can figure, boy."

Kate leaned forward in her chair. Her blue eyes were bright. "SSTs are leased to the government. Loaded by government people. The drivers are employed by the government. All checked out for character and so forth. Any local weight-watcher would have a hell of a time poppin' those seals."

"That's right, Kate," Joe said.

"But where does the mob figure in?" Barry asked.

"To take the heat off the real people behind it all," Kate said.

"Yeah," Barry said. "But if that's the case, it means some real FBI personnel are involved."

"Probably," Joe agreed. "The Bureau ain't what it used

to be, boy. Not like when Hoover run it. You got bad eggs all over government now.''

"Wait a minute, Dad. If one or two Bureau people are involved, they could easily keep their skirts clean in this thing. This is not a D.C. number. I think they're setting you up to take the fall if anything goes sour.''

"Might be. See why I wanted you out of it?''

So Big Joe had it figured out all along, Barry thought.

"It would be Fabrello and his people who took the first fall,'' Kate said. "And they'd start singing like birds, pulling all of us into the soup with them.''

"And the people at the bases would be clean,'' Barry said. "They'd say all they were doing was loading the stuff. It would be the responsibility of the person who put the seals on the doors who'd be in hot water.''

"The drivers,'' Kate said bitterly. "The drivers always get stuck with the last responsibility. Whoever is behind this thing is a rotten, no-good, dirty son of a bitch!''

Joe smiled thinly. "Kate, my dear. I agree with you. Now watch your mouth.''

7

"Something still doesn't add up," Barry said.

They had seen Joe Rivers to bed, waited until he was asleep, and returned to Kate's mobile home. Joe had close friends on either side of his house, and both families dropped in before Barry and Kate left, assuring the son they would look after the father.

"What doesn't?"

"The mob leaning on Dad that way. It just draws too much attention to them." Then he smiled grimly. "I'm not thinking clearly. Sure. Hell, they were ordered to do it. To make it appear more mob-oriented. To push whoever is really behind it further and further away from the heat."

"It's still a crappy thing to do. All the drivers are tryin' to do is make a living. As if the truck drivers don't have enough problems, now this."

"What do you know about Cottonmouth, Kate?"

"Forget it, Barry. He's straight. I been knowing that ol' boy for years."

"What's his real name?"

She grinned. "Shirley Hazelton."

Barry looked at her.

"I'm tellin' you, that's his name."

"I believe you. Nobody could make that up."

"So now you're my boss, right?"

Father and son had shaken hands on the deal after Big Joe called his attorney and explained what he wanted. The lawyer said he'd have the papers drawn up first thing in the morning.

"Looks like it. As soon as the papers are signed, I'll go over the roster of drivers and begin assigning partners."

"You're goin' ahead with this SST thing?"

"Hammer down."

"You gonna drive, Barry?"

"I damn sure am. I've still got my license and Dad gave me the keys to his rig."

"Who is your partner gonna be?"

"I haven't given it any thought." That was a lie.

"You can't lie worth a shit, boy!"

They looked at each other from across the room and both felt the silent click between them.

"You got to get cleared by those bogus FBI men before you can pull SSTs," she said.

"I've got a top-secret government clearance, Kate. That won't be any problem. If they denied me clearance, that would look awfully strange."

"And there's still the local mob to deal with."

"They don't worry me. What worries me is I don't know who to trust."

"What do you mean?"

"Washington people. Linda was awfully quick to ask me to do this."

"Who is Linda?"

"A friend of mine back in D.C. She works for the Justice Department."

"You two friends?"

"Yes. Nothing serious between us." A little screwing now and then is all.

But now there were seeds of doubt in his mind about her, and he wondered why.

"You thinkin' she has something to do with this mess?" she asked.

"I have no reason to think that. It's probably coincidence." He was conscious of Kate's eyes studying his face.

"It's gettin' late," Kate said.

"Yeah. You have a run tomorrow?"

"Just up to Alexandria. I may have to deadhead to Shreveport to pick up a backhaul. Damn near six of one and half a dozen of another when you consider the mileage."

"I wish I could go along," Barry said. "But . . ."

"You got papers to sign and a lot of catching up to do," she finished it. "How are those SSTs gettin' in here? Or are we pullin' our own?"

"By rail. They'll be here next Monday. That's when I get to meet one of those so-called FBI men."

"They slick," she said.

"Meaning they're intelligent?"

"That's what I said. That one that talked to me, he didn't miss a trick. He knew all the right questions and when to ask 'em."

Barry stood up. "I'd better go, I guess."

"You don't have to go." Kate's voice was husky, her eyes a smoky blue, clouded by flames from an inner fire.

"Is this wise, Kate?"

"I don't know about wise, Barry. I just know I want you to stay."

He reached over and turned off the overhead lights.

He left the trailer before dawn, returning to his motel room. He showered and shaved and dressed in jeans, western shirt, and cowboy boots. Then he drove to the terminal of Rivers Trucking.

A group of drivers was gathered on the docks, watching him as he pulled in. He noticed another plain sedan parked across from the terminal, just down the street. Two men sitting in the front seat, two men in the back.

Fabrello had beefed up his first team.

Barry shook hands with Jim, then motioned the drivers to gather around him on the docks.

"Big Joe is retiring. Not permanently; just until he gets back on his feet. I'm taking over. My name is Barry Rivers. I grew up in the cab of a truck, but I've been away from it for a long time. If I don't know something, I'll ask one of you about it. I expect straight answers and no bullshit." He noticed Kate, leaning against a crate, watching him. "There's a lot of things we need to talk about. But not now. Too many unfriendly eyes on us. And you know what I mean. And there may be unfriendly ears listening as well."

"What do you mean by that, Mr. Rivers?" a burly driver asked, stepping forward. "You mean one of us"—he waved at the group—"might be workin' for the other side?"

"There is that possibility," Barry said bluntly.

"I don't like nobody callin' me a sneak or a snitch," the driver said.

"Nobody did," Barry told him. "I implied that the possibility exists, that's all. I'll be talking to every one of you, one at a time, in private. And I'll be making damn sure you're either one hundred and ten percent for Rivers Trucking, or out on your ass. That's the way it's going to be. Anyone who objects to taking polygraph or PSE tests, haul your asses out of here—now.''

Not one driver moved. Barry's eyes touched them all. He noticed they were all, with the exception of Kate, forty years old or older. Not a hotdog or cowboy in the bunch—that he could spot. But he would check their records and driving later.

"I know the trouble you've been having. My dad is a proud man; he chose not to bring me in on it. I brought myself in. So let's clear the air, right now. I run this place. I sign your checks. You take orders from me. I'm not a hard person to get along with. I'm pretty easy, as a matter of fact. Until I'm crossed.

"If all goes well, we'll start pulling SSTs come Monday morning. At least we'll be picking them up at the railhead Monday morning. The ICC's OK'd the operating rights, and we'll get the bills of lading Monday, so I'm told. And I imagine some of us will be pulling out Tuesday morning. You've been briefed, but I'm going to brief you again. You'll be riding in pairs, so pick your partner . . .''

"You just said some of *us* will be pullin' out, Mr. Rivers,'' a driver said, stepping forward. "Does that mean you're gonna be drivin'?''

"It damn sure does.''

"Who's your codriver, Mr. Rivers?''

"Kate.''

The driver stepped back, nodded his head. Nothing else to say on that subject—and they all knew it.

Kate smiled faintly.

"Now,'' Barry said. "Let's clear the air on something.

No son of a bitch runs my drivers or my trucks off the road." His eyes found Chuck, the driver he'd overheard at the truck stop. The man standing next to him was Hank Grethal—Snake. "You two going to hang it up, boys?"

"I seen you at the truck stop, didn't I?" Chuck asked.

"Sure did."

"I'll stay for a few runs. See how things turn out," Chuck said.

"I'll stick around," Snake said.

"How many of you got runs today?" Barry asked.

All the drivers raised their hand, except for Jim Carson.

"What's the matter, Jim?" Barry asked with a smile. "Your reputation finally catch up with you?"

Jim grinned. "I figured someone ought to stick around and hold your hand. You been up near the Dirty Side for so long you might not know how to drive nothin' but a hog truck."

The drivers laughed and Barry grinned. "I'll drive circles around you any day, old man," Barry said.

"You might," Jim said. "Seein' as how me and Big Joe taught you ever'thing you know."

Barry waited until the laughter had died down. "Beginning right now, this run, you all go armed. I don't give a shit what the ICC says about it. You carry a pistol and shotgun with you, in the cab, at all times. You get stopped, I'll take the heat for it. You tell 'em those are company orders and to call me. I'll back you up a hundred and ten percent, and you do the same for me."

He met each man's eyes. No one backed down from his steady, hard gaze. "Take off."

Barry didn't trust the phones in his dad's office, so he told the secretary he'd be gone for about an hour. He drove around for a few minutes, noting the plain sedan following him. He twisted and turned and pulled into a parking garage. On foot, he managed to lose the men following him. He found a quiet phone booth and called his lawyer in D.C., using his credit card.

"Ralph? Your phone secure?"

"Wait a sec. It is now. What's going on, Barry?"

Barry brought the man up to date; what he knew and what he suspected.

"Jesus Christ!" the lawyer said. "You've stepped into a snake pit down there."

"I think so. Look, call the detective agency I use. You know who I'm talking about. Now tape this, Ralph." He looked at a small notebook and gave the lawyer the names of every driver and employee of Rivers Trucking. "I want them checked out from asshole to elbows and I want it done by Saturday morning—tops. OK?"

"They can do it. But it's gonna cost you."

"Whatever it takes. Just get it done. I don't trust the phones at the terminal or my dad's house, so I'll call you. Ralph, don't trust anybody in this thing. And I mean *anybody*."

"Looking back, Barry, it was a little bit easy for you, you know?"

"Looking back, I agree. Oh, by the way, my CB handle is Dog."

"Dog?"

"Dog."

"What's that mean?"

"It means I'll be driving a rig come Monday or Tuesday morning. So I might be a little hard to catch up with."

Silence on the line for a few seconds. "Barry, you've got a million-dollar consulting business. And you're going to be driving a *truck*?"

"I was a truck driver before I was anything else, Ralph."

"How wonderful for you." Ralph's reply was very dry. "I'm impressed."

Barry laughed at the man. "Get cracking, Ralph. I'll see you on the flip-flop."

"On the *what?*"

"Talk to you later, Ralph."

"The man has already forgotten how to speak English," Ralph muttered, then hung up.

When Barry got back to his office, Ted Fabrello was waiting for him.

8

The car he'd seen with the four toughs in it was gone. His secretary was behaving very oddly when Barry returned to the terminal. She kept motioning toward his office. Barry nodded in understanding. He had already seen the limo in the visitor's parking area and the two sedans beside it.

Barry didn't figure it was the mayor come to welcome him home personally. "Settle down," he told the woman.

"That's Ted Fabrello in there!" she hissed.

"Yeah? Well, then, I mustn't keep him waiting. Not someone that important."

Barry pushed open the door to his office and stepped inside. Ted Fabrello was sitting in the chair before his desk, a pair of muscle boys behind him. The muscle boys didn't worry him. He had learned a long time back that a well-placed bullet was worth several hundred pounds of muscle.

Like what that Maryland highway cop had told him once,

off the record, when asked what he would do if some two-hundred-and-eighty-pound ex-NFL tackle were to decide to attack him after being stopped for a traffic violation.

The highway cop had looked at him and said, "Blow his goddamn head off!"

Many cops operate under an unofficial motto: *I'd rather be judged by twelve than carried by six.*

Barry Rivers and Ted Fabrello looked at each other, silently sizing each other up. Barry thought the mobster was the ugliest bastard he'd ever seen. He had no idea what Fabrello was thinking and really didn't care.

"Since you probably think shaking my hand would be repugnant, I won't offer it," Fabrello said. His voice was well modulated, his speech free of any accent. It was obvious the man was well educated.

Barry stuck out his hand. "Oh, I'll shake your hand, Fabrello."

"*Mister* Fabrello," one of the apes said.

Barry smiled at the bodyguard. "Fuck you," he said sweetly.

Fabrello laughed until tears squeezed out of his buggy eyes. Wiping his eyes with a handkerchief, he said, "You really are a tough boy, aren't you, Rivers?"

"Only when I have to be." Barry sat down behind his desk and leaned back.

Fabrello turned his head and spoke to his two guards. "Take a hike, both of you. And shut the door on the way out."

Barry and Fabrello alone, Fabrello smiled. "Let's clear the air, Rivers. Then I can get on with my life, and you with yours. Agreed?"

"Fine."

"Good. Beneath your tough-boy exterior, you're a gentleman. I like that. Now then, I am not interested in your father's trucking business. I got trucking operations running out my ears. You wanna buy one? Cheap? I'll sell it. I have never used muscle against your father. I haven't used muscle against *anyone* in two years. That's the truth. This isn't the 1930s. There are other ways. Somebody has been dropping my name around town. Somebody has been saying that I'm muscling in on your father's business. I don't like that. It gives me a bad name. When I find out who is doing it, *then* I'm going to use muscle. I am going to break both their fucking arms—at the elbows—and both their fucking legs—at the knees. Then I am going to cut their balls off and stuff them in their mouths." He wiped his forehead with a handkerchief. When he looked up, Barry was smiling at him.

"You find my words amusing, Rivers?"

"No. I'm smiling because I think you're telling the truth."

"I *am* telling the truth. I got the Justice Department breathing down my neck about this trucking thing. And would you believe, for once, I'm *innocent!*"He leaned back in his chair and laughed. "Ain't that a hell of a note?"

"Then my father is in real danger, Fabrello. He's going to have to have round-the-clock protection."

"Then he's got it!" Fabrello said. "How many men you want? Ten—twenty? You name it, you got them. Hey! Blood is thick. I don't blame you for being hot. If my papa was still alive, some apes lean on him, I'll kill them. Consider your papa protected. From now on."

"All right." Barry was convinced the New Orleans capo was telling the truth. "And I thank you for that, Mister Fabrello."

The man's face brightened at the "Mister." "It's all right. But I ain't through. We got to talk some more."

Barry noticed the man's educated speech patterns came

and went from time to time, as he reverted to the streets. "As long as it takes."

"Those two goons you hammered on yesterday . . . you get a good look at them?"

"They weren't your men?"

"Hell, no! But I own that warehouse right across the street. Some of my people told me about this guy whipping the hell outta two much bigger men. I did some checking, found out it was you."

"Well . . . I tossed their car keys in that garbage can right there." Barry stood up and pointed. "Would that be of any help?"

"Might be." He called for his men and told them to bring the can over and dump it. Find the keys. He looked back at Barry. "New car?"

" '84 or '85 model, looked like."

"Good. If the keys are there, we can trace the key numbers. No sweat. OK, now let's talk about something else." He smiled. "You wanna hear something from a capo's mouth?" He laughed at Barry's startled expression. "Oh, sure, there are people who'll tell you the Mafia don't exist. Same people tell you the moon and tides don't affect broads neither. This conversation isn't leaving this office, Mr. Rivers. You and me, we both know that, don't we?"

Barry nodded. "Might take you a while, but you'd get me, right, Mr. Fabrello?"

"You're a smart man. I like that. I got to deal with a lot of dummies in business. I took a real chance coming to see you; I hope you appreciate that."

Again, Barry nodded.

"You see, Barry . . . mind if I call you Barry?"

Barry didn't mind.

"Good. I'm Ted. Not Teddy. I hate Teddy. My wife calls me Teddy. I hate my wife, too, but what the hell, you don't

wanna hear about her. *I* don't wanna hear about her. You
see, Barry, I'm what's known as middle-Mafia. I'm not the
old boys, and I'm not the young turks, neither. The old
boys would do anything—anything! Then we kicked them
out, took a look around, and said, *hey!* the old ways don't
get it—you know that I mean. So we backed off . . . ah,
certain projects. I don't do dope. No dope. Bad business.
Big money in it, but the risks are too great. I do women,
the waterfront, smuggling, car stripping, liquor, gambling/
numbers, I'm big in real estate and banks. That kind of
stuff. But no dope. And I don't fuck with the government.
I get audited every year. I'm clean, every year. Last two
years, they had to pay me some money. That pissed 'em
off, let me tell you."

He hitched his chair closer to Barry's desk. His smile
was conspiratorial. "But take a guess who is into dope."

"Certain people who work in various capacities for the
U.S. government."

Fabrello leaned back. "You're a *very* smart boy, Barry.
So why should I do all the talking? You tell me how you
got this scam figured."

Barry told him.

Fabrello nodded. "Right. Big Joe had it figured too,
didn't he?"

"Part of it. But he thought you were in it actively."

"No. I gotta go see that old bastard. 'Scuse my language;
didn't mean nothing by that. So you know what else I'm
gonna do? I'm gonna go to the FBI and tell them what I
know."

Barry shook his head. "No."

"No? No? What is with this no?"

"Because I think some FBI agents are involved in this
matter—on the other side."

Fabrello jumped to his feet. "That's disgusting. What

the hell is this country coming to—you can't even trust the FBI no more."

Barry waved him back to his seat. "Maybe half a dozen agents, tops."

"That's a relief." Fabrello paused. "What relief? What am I saying? Piss on the FBI. I hope they're all involved. That would be hysterical." He roared with laughter.

"Let's get back to something you said. What about these young turks?"

"Whole new story. They're into dope. They're into anything. They got their fancy college degrees and uptown educated women and they think they can't get caught. But they will. The whole country is beginning to get pissed off about dope. The Supreme Court is gonna turn around one of these days, soon, and the cops is gonna start kicking ass and taking names. Makes me nervous to even have prescription medicines in the house."

"And the young ones are . . . ?"

"No loyalty no more. It's disgusting. Yeah, they're part of this new thing. What you said, about the FBI . . . yeah, it's coming to me. There is some goddamn broad up there in Washington—with Justice—she's up to her ass in this thing. What the hell's her name. Irish broad, I think."

"O'Day."

"Yeah! How'd you know that?" He looked at Barry suspiciously.

"She's the one who told me about my dad. She . . ." Barry paused as bits and pieces of the puzzle began fitting. "Oh, yeah!," he said, disgust in his voice. "Tell me how you know about her."

"I got lawyers up there, man. I *gotta* have lawyers up there. But I can't figure this broad. I had her checked out, and she's one of them liberals. Now I love liberals, Barry. They're the best thing that's happened to guys like me since the ACLA. But her boyfriend is Bobby Bulgari. He's one of the new, young breed I was talking about. What the hell is a lawyer for the Justice Department doing screwing an up-and-coming mob boy? It don't figure."

It does to me, Barry thought. Linda needed a fall guy. So she picked me. And I don't believe for a minute she didn't know I was Big Joe Rivers's son. I just sprang it on her before she was ready, that's all.

"This Bulgari, he live in New Orleans?"

"Oh, yeah. Here and in Biloxi and in Aspen and several other places. But he's being groomed to take over when I retire. He . . ." Fabrello paused. His face darkened with rage. "Why, that son of a bitch! *He's* the one behind it all. I'll kill that no-good, lousy—"

"Wait a minute, Ted. I'm being used, you're being used, and I got a suspicion Bulgari is being used, as well."

"Oh, yeah? How do you figure that?"

Barry knew he wasn't going to tell the man about the SST contract; he had looked over the contracts and knew that would be a breach, and also there was no point in further endangering any of his drivers. "Look what a feather in her cap that would be, Ted. She breaks up a mob-run dope-smuggling ring—and you can bet there won't be anyone alive to testify against her; they'll be dead. She claims the credit for all the investigatory work. She's in the clear with a cool four- or five-million-dollar profit from the smuggled coke, and sitting in the catbird seat with a large promotion looking her in the face."

"And you and me and Bobby? . . ."

"Dead."

"I can understand me and Bobby, but why you, Barry?"

"You said it a minute ago, Ted: she's a screaming liberal. I'm in the arms business back in Maryland. I'm a consultant for the military, but I also own a large chunk of an import/

export business. I ship weapons of all types and calibers all over the world, and also bring them into this country for resale.''

Fabrello nodded his head. "And this O'Day broad—I seem to recall—has the hots for gun control. She's a peacenik. That word dates me, don't it? Yeah. OK. It's clear now. Barry," he said slowly, "you and me, we're in kind of a hard bind, you know that?''

"Yeah, that thought just came to me. If you were to go to your . . . well, colleagues with this information, it might be rubout time for you, for acting on your own without . . . committee approval, so to speak. 'Cause you can just bet that somebody close to the mob's inner circle is all ready with doctored phone tapes and notes, all implicating you, setting you up. As for me, I'd be willing to bet that Linda has a dossier on me, putting me right in the middle of this cocaine deal. Why else would a man leave a lucrative business to drive a truck? Tell you one thing, if Linda is the brains behind all this, she's slick.''

"Yeah. Well, you know what they say, Barry. The opera ain't over until the fat lady sings. I may be down, but I'm a hell of a long way from being counted out." He held up a big hand. "Don't worry, I'm not going to rock any boats; just do some very quiet snooping. Hey, your ass is in the same crack mine is in, Barry Rivers. You realize that, don't you?''

"Unfortunately."

Fabrello left Barry sitting quietly behind his desk, deep in thought. He had spoiled one part of Linda's plan by taping his visit with Treasury. Her name had been brought up several times, so if she had original thoughts of shifting blame from the Bureau over to Treasury, that was stymied . . . unless she could somehow get the tapes back.

No, he thought, she'd have to get the transcribed papers back as well. So that was out.

Barry knew he had no choice except to play along, see it through, and hope for the best.

9

Barry put everything out of his mind except the running of a trucking company. Friday morning, two FBI agents came to see him. They were friendly but businesslike, and their credentials were all in order. They were the genuine article.

Sure, Barry thought, these two would have to be, checking out the drivers of SSTs. The agents asked their questions, said there would be no trouble in getting Barry cleared—they knew who he was—then left, after handing Barry their cards. They were both out of the New Orleans office. Barry called the office and verified their employment.

Strange. If Linda was behind this mess, she was not averse to taking chances.

Then it came to him: how had the Bureau learned he was in New Orleans?

More unanswered questions.

Late Friday afternoon, the reports on the employees of Rivers Trucking came in by special messenger. Before he opened the thick package, Barry once again mulled over the matter of whether or not to tell the drivers the whole story.

They had a right to know. Not only their careers were on the line, but their lives as well.

He decided he would lay it on the line for them, but only after he read the reports.

He poured a fresh cup of coffee, opened the thick package, and leaned back in his chair, opening the first dossier.

An hour later, he was through. And satisfied. Every driver checked out. The detective agency had done their usual fine job, right down to listing the drivers' CB handles. No question about it, Barry had a group of steady, stable drivers working for him. Chuck and Snake were teaming up to drive together. Cottonmouth and Panty Snatcher. Beer Butt and Swamp Wolf. Bullwhip and Coyote. Saltmeat and Mustang. Cornbread and Grits. Beaver Buster and Lady Lou. Jim and Cajun. Dog and TNT.

Barry laughed softly.

It was good to be back home.

Using a pay phone in the lobby of a downtown hotel, Barry had reserved a meeting room at a small motel on Airline for Saturday night. Friday afternoon, Kate was the first driver back from her short run down to Houma. Barry waved her into his office and handed her the package of dossiers. She was not surprised; he had told her he was doing it.

She scanned the dossiers, then plopped them back on Barry's desk. "So everybody checks out. I figured they would. Now what?"

"You tell each driver when they pull in this afternoon we're having a meeting tomorrow night." He had checked his office for bugs and found none; the office was as secure as Barry could make it. "They don't tell their wives, girlfriends, husbands, or boyfriends where they're going. Stress that. I'm going to lay it all out for them tomorrow night. Some of them may decide to quit. If so, I sure won't blame them."

"It's getting dangerous now, isn't it, Barry?"

"Damn sure is."

For several hours a day, all that week, Barry had practiced with his dad's rig. A lot had changed since last he'd sat behind the wheel of a rig, but it didn't take him long to get back his touch. Years back, his father had told him he was a natural driver, and Barry had lost none of it.

His dad's rig was a midnight-blue Kenworth conventional with silver pinstriping. Smoked windows. The best sound system his dad could buy. Twin airhorns and twin remote-controlled spotlights. Forty-channel CB, SSB. Steer Safe stabilizers. Quartz halogen driving lights. Airglide 100 suspension. Alcoa aluminum ten-hold Budd wheels. Fuller Roadranger thirteen-speed transmission. The differentials were 3.73 Rockwells SQHP. Fontaine fifth wheel. Michelin steel-belt tires 1100x24.5 tubeless. Air dryer for air brakes. The mill was a 350 NTC Cummins with Horton fan clutch. Jake brake. The sleeper was a VIP walk-in, robin's-egg-blue interior, the bunk was an Electro-warmth mattress with mirrors and a twelve-volt TV.

His dad's favorite color must have changed from red to blue.

Barry had driven around the yard, spending hours practicing his backing until he felt he was ready. He knew his every move was being watched by the office workers and dispatch, and they would report to the drivers. They would know immediately if he couldn't cut it.

He had logged out on one short run, up to Baton Rouge. Two miles from the terminal, he knew he still had the touch and was ready.

But the word had gone out through the truckers' grapevine. Not many truckers wanted to chat with anybody from Rivers Trucking, and those that did were careful about what they said over the air. It wasn't fear on their part. More like a respect for the unknown.

The truckers were waiting to see what happened. They had all heard about the troubles of Rivers Trucking.

Confusing, Barry thought. I'm caught up in the middle of something that I don't fully understand. And it just didn't figure that Linda would dislike him enough to set him up for this kind of hard fall.

But it sure looked that way.

The drivers had all taken very twisting and confusing routes to the motel—at Barry's request. They knew the game was about to get very rough and dangerous.

They were a solemn bunch as they trouped in one by one and took their seats in the meeting room.

Barry closed and locked the doors and walked to the head of the long table. He looked at each serious face looking at him. There had been none of the usual kidding and horseplay among the drivers.

He laid it out for them, leaving nothing out. He told them about Fabrello's coming to see him. What they'd discussed. What they'd both concluded. He told them what he really did for a living, but said nothing of his Treasury connection. He did not tell them he was worth several million dollars. They probably would not have believed him anyway.

"That's it, people." Barry wound it down. "If anybody wants to quit, I sure won't hold it against them."

No one said anything for a full half-minute. Finally, Lady Lou raised her hand. Barry nodded at her. Lou was pushing fifty and had been a trucker for a quarter of a century. She and her husband had operated as independents for years, until economics forced them out. Her husband had been killed some years back, when he lost his rig on black ice and went over the high side in Utah. Lou was an attractive woman, her hair streaked with gray that she wore proudly. She was also as tough as a boot and had decked more than one driver who'd gotten too mouthy.

"It looks to me like somebody got the red-ass at you, Mr. Rivers," she said.

"Sure does," Barry said. "But I think that's only a small part of the big picture. What it boils down to is this: somebody is out to make a couple of million bucks and they've worked out a damn good plan to do it. And they don't care who gets hurt or killed in the process. They've gone to a lot of trouble to cover their butt. And set other people up to take the heat should the plan fall apart along the way."

"Yeah," Cajun said. "And those other people is *us*. We're the ones got to put those seals on the doors. I tell y'all what. This pisses me off."

"Sure was quiet out on the slab today," Saltmeat said. "Made me feel awful lonesome."

"Made me feel like a redheaded stepchild," Beer Butt observed.

Barry let them talk. He was sure about Jim, Kate, Cottonmouth, Chuck, and Snake. The others? He didn't know.

Barry unlocked the doors and waved the waitresses into

the room. They came in carrying trays of ribeyes, baked potatoes, salads, pie, and iced tea.

The drivers said nothing until the waitresses had left and the doors were once more locked. They talked as they ate.

"Runnin' SSTs, we're authorized to carry weapons, right, Mr. Rivers?" Bullwhip asked.

"M-16s, shotguns, and sidearms."

"I'll see it through," he said. "There ain't no son of a bitch gonna make me quit drivin'."

His partner, Coyote, nodded in agreement. "Yeah, me, too."

"When do we get checked out with weapons?" Beaver Buster asked.

"We don't."

The drivers digested that bit of news. Beaver Buster said, "You can count me in. I'm stayin'." He looked at his partner, Lady Lou. "How 'bout you?"

"I'm in," she said.

Mustang said, "You know, somebody real high up is involved in this mess. I know guys who work SSTs. They've all been through weeks of trainin'. Most of them are ex-Green Berets, ex-Rangers, ex-Marines, ex-Paratroopers . . . outfits like that. And to just hand us automatic weapons and toss us out . . ." He shook his head. "That's crap. But I'm curious, so I'm stayin'."

"You never did have no sense," Saltmeat said, looking at his partner. "So I guess I'd better throw in and come along. Somebody's got to look after you."

"I'll check you out with the M-16s," Barry said. "But I imagine most of you have fired them."

The drivers smiled. Barry knew they were familiar with the weapon.

"Yeah," Cornbread said. "But it's been a long time since I fired one."

"It don't make no difference," his partner, Grits, said. "You can't hit nothin' anyway."

"Yeah," Beer Butt said. "And if you can't shoot no better than you drive, we're all in trouble."

"I was in the Army!" Cornbread said.

"Yeah," Swamp Wolf said. "In the motor pool."

"I didn't even know you could swim," Mustang said.

Barry relaxed and let them insult each other. They were all staying.

He looked over at Kate. She smiled at him. He winked at her and she returned the wink. She was not a good winker, screwing up the entire side of her face. Made her look like a pixie.

Barry wondered if any of them really knew just how dangerous the job was that faced them all. He decided they did. And they weren't staying because of the increase in pay, which was considerable. Truckers are a hardy, stubborn breed—the last cowboys. There is not a rig they can't drive or a road they can't run. Tell them they can't, and they'll show you they can. This present situation was insulting to them; not just to them personally, but to a way of life. To the whole, loose-knit fraternal organization of truckers.

Beer Butt looked at Barry. "You gonna eat that apple pie?" he asked.

"Uh . . . no," Barry said.

"Good," Beer Butt said, reaching over and taking the pie. "My momma taught me to clean my plate."

"And anybody else's that happens to be near," Panty Snatcher remarked.

10

Barry arranged the use of a small privately owned firing range, and at one o'clock Sunday, the drivers gathered there.

It really didn't come as any surprise to Barry that all the men were familiar with the M-16, or that many had owned one in the past. Many truckers are outdoorsmen, hunters, fishermen, and very much the individualist. They don't give a flying fart what federal law dictates about guns. If they want to carry a gun, they'll carry a gun.

As should be the case for any taxpaying, normally law-abiding citizen who knows the law is slanted toward the criminal and against them.

Barry checked them out first with the M-16. For all their penchant for joking, the drivers took the gun training very seriously, without their usual bantering and horseplay. All the men had their own pistols, and most there preferred the bigger pistols: the .357s and the .44 mags. Barry had never liked those pistols; his choice of a handgun had been, for years, the 9mm, models 39 or 59. But if the other drivers were more comfortable with the larger calibers, and could hit what they were shooting at, fine.

Lady Lou could handle the twelve-gauge shotgun, but Kate was so small, she had difficulty with it. Barry gave her a twenty-gauge magnum and she found she could handle it much better. She was also a good shot with a .38. But when the little blonde grabbed the new model M-16 and cut loose, every driver there hit the ground. And stayed there until Barry took it from her.

Barry knew he could not teach Kate what she needed to know about the M-16. She was nervous about handling the unfamiliar weapon, and that was working against her.

Barry had her concentrate on the pistol and shotgun for the remainder of the afternoon.

He called a halt to the practice at five o'clock. "We pick up the SSTs at eight o'clock in the morning," he told the group. "I open the rolling orders as soon as we're back at the terminal. I'll see you all at the terminal at seven o'clock. Those M-16s are signed out in your names. Be careful. They're probably hot government property."

As he expected, everyone got a laugh out of that.

"You really think these weapons are hot?" Snake asked.

"It wouldn't surprise me," Barry told him. "Like I said, and you all agreed, we're being set up for a fall. And it could come at any time."

"Real nice people behind all this crap," Beaver Buster said.

"Yeah," Barry said. "Just peachy."

Barry had requested some information about SSTs from a local library. He couldn't get very much about it, and that also came as no surprise. But what he did get made him realize all the more how much they were being set up for a hard fall.

About a year back, there were fewer than sixty SSTs rolling in America. Barry thought he could accurately add ten more to that number. The "Suicide Jockeys," as they are called by other truckers, log about five million miles per year, calling on more than 130 destinations within the continental U.S.

Their rigs are designed to look like other rigs. They obey all the speed limits and traffic laws. They want no undue attention brought to their top-secret shipments.

They work for the U.S. Department of Energy, Transportation Safeguards Division.

Well, Barry thought about the IDs issued them—so far, so good.

The Suicide Jockeys may be pulling inactivated atomic or hydrogen bombs, nuclear cannon shells, weapons-grade uranium or plutonium, top-secret trigger parts for hydrogen bombs. They might be hauling ammunition, grenades, nerve gas, tear gas . . . anything that's dangerous and deadly.

The SSTs are heavily armored and manned by what the Energy Department calls "couriers." The drivers, or couriers, are described as civilian Green Berets; the most ready-for-combat contingent in the nation. Sometimes they ride three to a cab: two up front, one in the sleeper. If it is a long-haul run, there are usually four or five other couriers rolling along with them in unmarked cars or pickups.

The men—and they are almost always men—are always U.S. armed forces vets. They have what is known as a Q clearance, the Energy Department's highest security clearance.

With the exception of Barry's drivers, they are tested and trained rigorously for anywhere from eight to sixteen weeks. They are trained to cope with everything from helicopter attacks or light-armored vehicle assaults to a nut in a ditch with a rocket launcher, hijackers, or blockades.

It is the most expensive trucking line—for its size—in the world. Its operating budget the year the article was written reached fifty million dollars. To replace an SST would cost nearly a million dollars.

What Barry read next chilled him and brought home just how vulnerable he and his drivers were going to be. And how dangerous was the setup.

Supposedly, the tractors have beefed-up safety features. Their windshields are bulletproof; the added armor plating is three-inch-thick slab steel. Walls, ceilings, and floors are steel-armored, insulated, and fireproof. If a rig is attacked during transport, a button can be pushed, locking the axles so that only a cutting torch can free them.

Naturally, none of the Rivers's rigs had any of that.

The shipping containers of the SSTs have been designed for the worst type of accident. They have been tested through fire, immersion, and free fall. The shipping containers must emerge tied down and in place and intact after simulated sixty mph head-on crashes.

Barry glanced at his watch just as Kate was walking into the terminal office. Six A.M. Monday morning.

"You're early," he said with a smile. "I thought I left you sleeping."

"I got up right after you did," the petite blonde said. "The bed got lonesome."

He handed her the report he'd been reading.

She quickly read the brief report and tossed it back on his desk. "Well, I damn sure don't have none of that on my rig."

"Nor do I on Dad's. I wish you'd—"

"Forget it!" she cut him off, guessing what he was going to say. "I'm a truck driver. I'll take my chances just like the rest."

No surprise. "Hungry?"

"I could eat an armadillo!"

"I think we can come up with something a bit more appetizing than that."

The two men who met the drivers at the railroad pickup point handed Barry a thick sealed envelope. Barry signed for the packet and the men turned around and walked off. Not one word had been exchanged.

"Friendly types, ain't they?" Beaver Buster remarked.

"You ought to feel right at home with them," Cottonmouth said. "Seein' as how that's the way your mother-in-law treats you all the time."

"Looks about like that ol' boy, too," Beaver Buster observed.

"I know them things ain't loaded," Bullwhip said. "So where do we pick up the shipments?"

"It's all in here," Barry said, holding up the thick envelope. "Let's get those piggybacks off and hooked up."

Kate looked up at him. "Deadhead all the way to Arizona?" she whispered, remembering Big Joe's words about the shipments. "That don't make sense, Barry. This train could have dropped the trailers off there."

"I know. Maybe we're wrong, Kate. Maybe the dope is already hidden and we're taking it out of there. But that doesn't make sense either. We'll just have to play it by ear."

Back in his office, Barry looked over the contents of the packet. Instructions, bills of lading, bonds of indemnity, certificates of insurance . . . all the necessary documents; and they were legitimate. At least they appeared so. He let the other drivers scan the documents. They all verified the papers' authenticity.

For all their butchering of the English language, sounding as though their education had stopped at kindergarten, Barry knew a lot of that was deliberate on the part of the drivers. He knew that Beer Butt had a degree in business from the University of Alabama; Chuck was a former school teacher; Cajun had been a jet pilot in Vietnam, flying C-130s . . . and so on down the line.

"We roll out at six in the morning," Barry said. "Five units. Kate and me, Chuck and Snake, Cottonmouth and Snatcher, Beaver Buster and Lou, Beer Butt and Swamp Wolf. The rest of you will be in cars and pickups. Jim, you and Cajun will drive my pickup. The rest of you will be in the car provided by the government. We don't have a choice in the route; that's been preset by someone else. I don't even like to think who. We'll be heading to Fort Huachuca, Arizona. We'll pick up a load, and take it to Nevada. Before you ask, I don't know where in Nevada. We'll be told that at Huachuca. Right now, let's all take a look inside those trailers."

None of them had ever seen anything like it. Barry sensed the moment he swung open the doors and stepped inside that this was the genuine article: a government SST.

"Look at these walls," Grits exclaimed. "You couldn't punch through them with a fifty-caliber machine gun."

Each trailer was slightly different from the others. Each designed for a certain type of cargo.

"At least there ain't no tanker," Lou said. "That's a relief."

They all knew what she meant and silently agreed with her.

Barry had stepped outside and was going over the route. Every mile of the way was spelled out. There would be no detours or deviations allowed. Every stop was clearly marked.

Why? he thought. When we're deadheading? He could understand that when pulling a load. He shrugged it off.

The small convoy would follow Interstate 10 all the way, leaving the interstate just a few miles north of the military base and taking a two-lane down to the base.

About thirteen hundred miles. And there would not be a mile that went by without wondering what is around the next curve? What's over that next hill? How will *they* do whatever it is *they* are going to do?

And when?

11

The convoy pulled out at dawn on Tuesday morning. With Barry and Kate in the front door, followed by Chuck and Snake, Cottonmouth and Snatcher, Jim and Cajun in Barry's pickup, Beaver Buster and Lou, Saltmeat and Mustang and Cornbread and Grits in a four-door Mercury, then Beer Butt and Swamp Wolf, with Bullwhip and Coyote filling the back door in a second pickup truck.

All the vehicles were CB-equiped, with the government car and pickup's two-way high-bands equipped with scrambler on both ends. Those radios were in addition to CBs. The high-band-equipped vehicles would not stay in any assumed position within the convoy. They would be ranging, from time to time, far out in front and far back in the drag. They would use the high-band radios to warn each other in case of trouble. Not that they were really needed. With illegal wattage boosters on each CB, kicking the CBs up from four watts to one hundred watts of power, the truckers could very nearly communicate with a goat herder in Greece. Providing the goat herder had a CB.

The convoy pulled off at Lake Charles for food and fuel. Barry had taken the first trick at the wheel; Kate would take it from Lake Charles to just outside of San Antonio. The convoy had been running at a steady rate of sixty mph; in most states they were safe at that speed, and even at that, nearly everyone was passing them.

After eating and fueling, the latter something that is required by law, they checked in at the local weight-watcher's rip-off and rolled on into Texas.

"Now it's about to get boring," Kate said.

Barry looked at her.

"Miles and miles of nothin' but miles and miles," she said with a smile. "It's not so bad around here. But just wait until we get past San Antonio."

The hours and miles rolled on. Light melted into dusk and twilight drifted into night, split only by the beams of headlights. The convoy kept chatter on the CB to a minimum.

All in all, Barry thought, it's a boring run. Then he remembered something. "Kate, is there a punch set in this rig?"

She smiled. "Oh, I imagine we could come up with one. Why?"

"I want to search these containers. And we're not going to be able to do that on the bases."

"True. But what you're thinking is risky, Barry."

"Sure. But do we have a choice?"

"No. I got a bunch of blank seals."

"My, my!"

They made the run in just over thirty hours; no record by anyone's count. The guards at the front gate checked their papers, then gave them instructions to the warehouse row—with an armed escort.

"Relax," a lieutenant told Barry after the SSTs had been backed up to the docks. "Coffee in there," he pointed. "We'll load it up and seal it for you."

"You load 'em up," Barry said. "We'll check it and witness the seal."

The lieutenant gave him a strange look. "Whatever you say, driver."

"Where are we taking this load?"

"This your first run with SSTs?"

"Yes."

"I thought so. Come on, we'll go over your route."

In his office, the officer pulled out a map. "Short run this time," he said, punching a spot on the map. "Right here. Yuma Proving Grounds. Go back the way you came and take 10 West. Take Interstate 8 to Yuma, then cut north on 95. As soon as you get within the perimeter of the grounds, you'll be met. Password is Gold Star. Your response is Poppyseed. You got that?"

"I got it. And if they don't know the right password?"

The officer's gaze was bleak. "Shoot them and get the hell out of that area. Get on your radios and start hollering."

So it had all been changed since Big Joe was contacted. Barry wondered about that, but decided to keep his mouth shut. He had no way of knowing if this officer was part of whatever was going down, or whether he was straight.

But what if this was a test of some sort? Barry looked at the young lieutenant.

"Something on your mind, driver?"

"I thought we were taking this load to Nevada?"

"Yeah? Well, so did I. Word came down the line yesterday. You got a change in plans. Don't worry, I've got all the papers you'll need. Everything is in order." He grinned. "You'll get used to this. It happens all the time. That should tell you right off that you're not hauling anything hazardous. Anything hazardous and your route would be spelled out tight."

"What are we hauling?"

The lieutenant shrugged. "Partner, I don't have any idea."

Whatever they were hauling was going to remain a mystery to the truckers, and they all knew it as soon as the complicated seals were in place.

Kate whispered to Barry, "No way we can pop those seals and replace them."

"Yeah." But an idea was forming in his mind.

When they were clear of the base and heading north toward Interstate 10, Barry said, "I think those seals just kicked the drug-smuggling idea in the head, Kate."

"At least as far as blaming it on us," she replied.

"So, now what? Give me your thoughts."

"I don't have any—wait a minute. How do we know all the seals are going to be the same? I've never pulled SSTs before. Each base may have their own type of seal, depending on the cargo."

"So we keep on truckin' and hope for the best, right?" he said with a smile.

"You got any better ideas?"

"Not a one."

The convoy stopped just outside of Yuma for food and fuel and to wait for the dawn. They could not deliver at night. Too risky, the lieutenant said. Too much of a chance for a screwup.

Barry walked around the rigs in the predawn darkness, deep in thought. He squatted down, his back to a wheel, and reviewed the fast-paced events in his mind.

Had Fabrello been telling the truth? The capo had indeed put guards around his father's house . . . very discreetly. He had even met with Big Joe and apologized for the behavior of Bulgari. No, Barry felt Fabrello was telling the truth.

After speaking with Fabrello, Barry had called his attorney in D.C. and asked him to put the detective agency on Linda; see what they could come up with. From a truck stop in Texas, Barry had called Ralph. Again, Fabrello had been speaking the truth. Linda was very quietly seeing Bobby Bulgari whenever the two of them could chance it. Most recently, she had spent a weekend with him at his condo in Biloxi, flying down to meet him in a private Lear jet.

Who owned the jet?

The agency was working on that.

But she had sure been sneaky about it, traveling in disguise. Wig, dark glasses, different style of dress, different makeup.

Barry had to wonder if she could be doing this in order to gain more evidence against Bulgari and the mob.

He rejected that and so did the detective agency and his attorney.

Linda O'Day was up to her ass in something big and dirty and illegal. Or was she?

And everybody Barry had spoken with seemed to think it was dope. They also thought Barry was being set up to take the heat and the fall at some point along the line.

When?

No one knew.

Barry stood up and stretched. He leaned against the trailer, the side of his face against the dew-coolness of metal. A little door in his mind opened, allowing more light to shine on the mystery he'd pondered over.

Not the trailer. Not the contents. That would require too many people to make it work. Linda would have to have two or more people at every pickup point for it to jell. More than two, probably. And Barry doubted that many servicemen and women—who had been checked out by several security agencies—could be bought.

Not the trailer. Not the contents.

Then . . . where?

In the tractors, probably. Maybe in the storage areas. In the mattress, the trim, the upholstery, the vents, the padding. A dozen different places.

And if it was dope, it did not have to be placed at the SST's pickup points—not really. Rigs are not that difficult to break into. Any moderately competent lock man could easily slip into one of the tractors, plant the stuff, and be gone, all in the time it took the driver to eat a meal. Or, for that matter, the dope could have been planted while the rigs were back at the terminal.

Shit.

Now what to do?

When everyone had awakened, Barry called them off to one side and told them of his suspicions.

"I should have thought of that when I saw those seals back at the base," Cottonmouth said.

"I been kickin' this around in my head," Lou said. "And now that you've come up with your idea, hear mine. I think this proximity to Mexico is just another ruse to cover another trail."

Beaver Buster looked at her. "You wanna explain that?"

"If you'll shut your trap. Look here, New Orleans is one hell of a big port. And it was stupid, to my way of thinking, to hook up in New Orleans and deadhead all the way out to the base. I think the dope was planted back at the terminal and we've still got it with us. And 95, from Yuma to the Proving Grounds, is one hell of a desolate stretch. Right?"

"What you're saying about New Orleans is that the dope comes in through there?" Barry asked.

"Right. And how do we know the people who are supposed to meet us are on the up-and-up? This whole thing could be set up back in Washington and these Army types completely innocent. Whoever set this up is gonna have access to the code words."

All agreed with that. This was no longer Barry's show alone. They were all involved, and all had a right to his or her say.

"All right, people," Barry said, when no more opinions or suggestions were forthcoming. "Let's get some breakfast and hit it. When we turn off on 95, heads up. We may just be making a run to drop off cargo. And then again . . ."

He trailed it off. He did not have to say more. SST drivers don't carry guns for show.

12

The convoy headed straight north on 95. From Interstate 8 to Interstate 10, it was eighty-one miles of near desolation. And the old gut feelings that Barry used to experience in 'Nam had returned like a long-lost love reentering his life.

The small convoy was surrounded by the desert's mountains. To their left, the west, lay the Trigo and Chocolate mountains. To their right, the east, lay the Castle Dome, the Palomas, and a bit to the north and east, the Kofa Mountains. And all around them, no signs of life.

Barry's truck led the way, Kate behind the wheel. Her eyes had widened when Barry pulled the Uzi out of its case and fitted a clip into its belly.

"What kind of a gun is *that*?" she asked.

"Uzi. Best little submachine gun going, in my opinion." He lifted his eyes as they approached a picnic and camping area. Two Jeeps sat parked side by side. "There they are. Let me handle the show, Kate."

"You're more than welcome to it."

A man stepped out from under the wheel of one of the Jeeps and waved the convoy to a halt. Barry stepped down and rounded the truck, the Uzi in his right hand, held by the grip, his finger off the trigger.

The officer's eyes widened slightly at the sight. "Mr. Rivers," he said. "You don't believe in taking chances, do you?"

"I don't believe that's the password, Captain."

"No, it isn't. You're quite right. How about Gold Star?"

"Poppyseed."

"Good." The captain smiled. "Now we can be friends. If you will mount up and please follow us, Mr. Rivers."

"Not just yet."

The captain turned slowly. His face was flushed and his eyes angry. "What do you mean?"

"Let me see your ID. All of you." His finger had slipped into the trigger of the Uzi.

"The password and the response were correct. That is all you need, Rivers."

"And I'm curious as to how you know my name."

Barry heard the sounds of the other drivers climbing down from their rigs, guns in their hands. He heard Kate say, "Three more vehicles off to the east, Barry. Three, four men to a car. They're gettin' out, walkin' this way."

"We'll take care of the new boys, Barry," Saltmeat spoke.

"Now look here!" the captain—if that's what he was— spoke. "This is getting out of hand. You goddamn truck drivers are taking all this a bit too seriously. Now you eighteen-wheel cowboys just climb back in your rigs and follow me. And by God, that's an order!"

Barry felt the other drivers stiffen with sudden anger.

He heard Lady Lou say, "That son of a bitch needs an attitude adjustment."

The captain—again, if that's what he was, and Barry had serious doubts about that—did not know much about truck drivers. But if he didn't watch his mouth, he was going to find out. The hard way.

"Just show me your military ID, Captain," Barry told him. "Then everything will be just dandy."

The captain smiled and nodded to the men standing behind him. A signal? Barry wondered. He thought so. But a signal to do what? He'd soon know.

The captain moved his hand closer to the butt of his holstered .45. The flap was not secured. "I think, Rivers, you are making a very big mistake. You're under contract to the government, and out here, I represent the government."

"Just show me your ID."

"I'll show you this!" The man jerked out his .45.

Barry shot him just as the man pulled the trigger of the .45. The .45 slug whined off the barren earth. Barry's slugs took the man in the stomach and chest, knocking him backward, flinging him to the hot earth.

Jumping backward and rolling on the ground, Barry yelled, "Cover!"

The hot morning erupted in gunfire as the captain died, his blood quickly soaking into the sand.

Kate lifted her shotgun and tore the guts of one man into magnum-pounded bits of blood and flesh. The man was lifted from his feet and hurled to the ground. He screamed and rolled on the sand, then passed out.

"Bullwhip!" Barry shouted over the din of the battle. "Get on the horn and call in. Tell them we're under attack."

Barry raised his Uzi and cut the legs from under a man,

noting as he did so that the man's shoes were not military-issue.

Barry heard a man call out: "We only got a couple of minutes to get this done. Finish 'em, goddammit!"

One man, dressed in a military uniform but carrying a non-military-issue AK-47, charged at the convoy, the AK spitting and yammering. Barry swung his Uzi and pulled the trigger just as Lady Lou triggered off a burst from her M-16. 9mm and 5.56mm slugs struck the man and sent him sprawling to the ground, the AK's muzzle digging a hole in the sand.

"No go, no go!" a man screamed. "Back off. Let's get the hell outta here!"

Beer Butt shot him in the center of the chest with a .41 magnum, punching a thumb-sized hole going in and a fist-sized hole when the slug exited out the man's back, tearing the spinal cord. The man dropped to the ground, as limp and lifeless as a doll flung to the floor.

Barry burned a full clip at the back of a car as it roared away, rear tires spinning in the sands, throwing up clouds of dust. He saw the rear window shatter as the slugs punched through the glass.

Silence. Broken only by nervous coughing and the clearing of throats. Kate bent double and vomited on the ground. Lou ran to her side and put an arm around her waist, leading her away, behind a truck.

"Check your weapons!" Barry called. "Reload and stand ready." The incident had flung him back in time, back to the jungles and marshes and rice fields of 'Nam. "Eyes open, people."

He cautiously checked the fallen men. One was still alive, but he wouldn't be for long. His chest was pockmarked with bullet holes, his mouth leaking pink saliva. Lung shot.

The man drummed his heels on the hot ground and then died.

In the distance, Barry could hear the sounds of sirens. He could see the dust fanning out behind the approaching vehicles.

"Take cover!" Barry shouted. "Watch your perimeters; at the ready."

"Sounds like a fuckin' drill sergeant," Panty Snatcher muttered as he slipped under a trailer, assuming the prone position.

The cars and Jeeps slid to a halt. A young man dressed in field clothes, desert cammies, jumped out and faced the front of the convoy. Barry was kneeling by the side of his Kenworth, the Uzi ready. The officer held his hands out, showing he was friendly.

"Password!" Barry called.

"Gold Star."

"Poppyseed. Toss your ID on the ground and stand back."

The officer, a lieutenant, tossed his ID to the sands and stepped back. Barry picked up the plastic-sealed ID and checked it. It looked legit. The picture matched the face. He handed the ID back to the man.

"I'm Barry Rivers. I don't know who these dead men are."

"We're about to find out, Mr. Rivers. We were rolling to intercept you when we heard your trouble call." He turned to a sergeant. "Notify the highway patrol. Block off this highway north and south. Call the base. Tell them I want CID out here, right now. Tell them to notify the FBI and the DOT. Move it."

* * *

If there was any traffic that wanted to move north or south on 95 that morning, they were out of luck. The state police and MPs were in place within minutes, blocking the highway. A bird colonel came in by helicopter and took charge.

"There will be no press on this, Mr. Rivers," he told Barry. "These things don't happen often, but they have happened. We don't allow press on the incidents."

Obviously, the colonel and Barry shared the same opinion of many of the nation's press types.

"I understand and quite agree, Colonel."

"I thought you would, Colonel," the colonel said dryly. Obviously, he had done some checking on Barry.

Barry smiled. "Laos, 1968. Right, Colonel?"

The man smiled. "Right. But we were both a long way from birds, then. Good to see you. I want to talk to you after this mess is cleared up. Right now, let's see what it is you're carrying that is so important."

Barry stared at the man. "You don't *know*?"

"I have no idea, Barry," the officer admitted. "All I know is that Rivers Trucking is bringing cargo to this drop-off point to be disposed of." He smiled. "Government rules and regs, buddy. The business you're in back in Maryland, you should be familiar with them."

So he had been checked out—but why? "Quite," Barry said.

Barry never did discover what he had been hauling. The reinforced and sealed containers were removed from the trailers and trucked away by soldiers. The brief and bloody combat area was cleaned up within an hour, with no sign of any struggle left for curious eyes. Highway 95 was reopened for civilian traffic and Barry and his people moved onto the Proving Grounds. Kate and the others were escorted to one camouflaged blockhouse; Barry and the colonel went to another. Both were comfortable and air-conditioned, with tables and bunks and offices.

The colonel waved Barry to a seat and poured them both mugs of coffee. "OK, Mr. Rivers," he said. "It's leveling time. What in the hell is a millionaire arms consultant and dealer, a bird colonel in a Green Beanie outfit, doing driving a goddamned truck?"

"I might ask why you know so much about me." Barry countered.

"SST drivers get checked from asshole to elbows, Barry. Even in a hurry-up operation like this one seems to be."

"I was wondering if the swiftness of all this might have come to your attention."

"Not just my attention, but the attention of several people very high up in this nation's security." He paused, waiting.

Barry waited him out and down, remaining silent, watching the officer.

The colonel sighed. "I never did like cloak-and-dagger shit, Barry. That's why I went back to being a line officer. Believe me, I *did not* ask for my present assignment. I suppose it's what we both get for being A-Team men in our crazy youth." His smile was filled with irony.

"You understand my reluctance to discuss this with you, then?" Barry asked.

"Yes, I suppose so. Those men who attacked your convoy were not carrying any IDs. If they've ever been fingerprinted, we'll find out who they are—eventually. But as you know only too well, it's not as easy as the movies depict it. Without compromising yourself, or what you believe or suspect to be happening, what can you tell me?"

"We were attacked."

The officer lost his temper. "Oh, come off it, goddammit! The Pentagon sent me your whole goddamn jacket, Colonel. They're just as curious as I am about why you're doing this. I'll level with you, Colonel, whether or not you decide to play it straight with me. CID and ASA people started checking as soon as your name popped up as an SST driver. Somebody is pulling one hell of a scam— for want of a better word—down in New Orleans. I think one CID man called it a double-double-cross. It has more twists in it than a bag full of snakes. We know that somebody tried to make it appear that a local mobster named Fabrello was muscling in on your dad's trucking business. But Fabrello doesn't have a damn thing to do with it. It appears that a lieutenant in the Dixie Mafia, somebody named Bulgari, has a pipeline into and out of some government agencies in D.C. It also appears that we have anywhere from two to six renegade government agents, possibly from the FBI and the Justice Department. But we don't know who they are. Do you?"

Barry shook his head. "No. I don't know who the agents are." Not a lie, for he didn't know any of the agents. Just Linda O'Day.

"That was a neat trick you pulled with Treasury, Colonel. Very cute. But I'm not sure how smart a move it was."

"Meaning? . . ."

"You just might be a prime target for a setup. Are you aware of that possibility?"

"Yes. I believe it was the original plan by . . . somebody."

"But you don't know who that person might be?"

"I don't have a clue, Colonel. That's just one of the reasons I'm in this thing. To find out, if I can."

The officer stared at Barry. Barry could tell the man didn't believe him. But who could he trust? Barry had no way of knowing who in the field might be involved in this matter.

"All right, Colonel Rivers," the officer sighed. "Play it

your way. If you ever get around to trusting me, give me a call. I'll do what I can to help you."

"I'll bear that in mind. And thank you."

"I have your traveling orders."

"Where do we go from here?"

"Not we, Mr. Rivers. Just one truck with no escort. The rest of your people will proceed to the Desert Range Test Station in Utah. They'll wait for the single truck there, while they're being loaded. I get this feeling you'll be driving the lone rig up to northern California?"

"You got that right, Colonel. Where in northern California?"

"The government has a small . . . test facility just south and west of Redding. Very small facility; very top secret. You'll pick up some . . . material there." He handed Barry several small envelopes. "Good luck, Colonel."

"Am I going to need it?"

"Probably."

Barry didn't like the sound of that at all.

13

"We must be going to haul perishables, Barry," Kate said, when Barry emerged from the blockhouse.

"Perishables? What are you talking about?"

"While you were in there talkin', I was told to unhook one SST and hook up to a reefer."

"Frozen-food trailer?"

"No. It's a medium-temp reefer. We could backhaul dry freight in it. Right over there," she said, pointing.

Barry could hear the refrigeration unit running. "They must want it cold when we get there."

"Said they did. I asked what we'd be haulin'. Soldier said he didn't know. He was just followin' orders."

At once, Barry thought of temperature-controlled explosive compounds, like nitro, which can get neither too hot nor too cold. But he rejected that within seconds after thinking it.

He looked around. The soldiers had worked fast at

unloading; the Rivers trucks were empty and ready to roll, the containers off-loaded onto military trucks and already gone.

"Yeah," Kate read his thoughts. "They sure don't tarry."

Barry waved his people over to the hot shade of a trailer.

"Any word on who those guys were?" Cottonmouth asked.

Barry shook his head. "Not yet. Maybe never. OK, we have our traveling order. Kate and me, with no escort, will be heading up to northern California. The rest of you will head to Utah." He handed Jim his sealed orders. "It's all in there. You're to wait for us. I don't know what we're picking up; I don't know what you're picking up."

"How come the reefer?" Beer Butt asked.

"There again," Barry said, "I don't know. Your route is all marked out. You know the rules. Take off."

Jim hesitated.

"Something on your mind, Jim?" Barry asked.

"I don't like the idea of us splittin' up," he said flatly.

"Neither do I. But I don't know anything we can do about it. For what it's worth, I think the colonel here is on the level. But I didn't level with him; for obvious reasons."

"Barry," Coyote said. "Who can any of us trust in this?"

"Each other. And no one else."

Kate took the first trick at the wheel after reviewing the preplanned route. "They sure got us routed funny," she said. "But the government's payin' the bills, so here we go."

Barry and Kate took 95 north, up to Interstate 10, then cut west. The logical route would be to stay on the interstate, but their orders were to pick up 95 again just east of Blythe and take that up to Interstate 40 at Needles, then cut west.

"That's about a hundred miles of nothing," Barry noted. "Stay at the wheel. I'll ride shotgun until we hit the interstate."

"If they're going to hit us, Barry—whoever they might be—they might be thinking that after we clear 95, we'll relax. You ever driven 40 miles from Needles to Barstow?"

"No."

"About a hundred and forty miles of nothing. It's interstate, but they could hit us there just as easily."

Barry looked at the map and grimaced. "You're right. Well, we're flying by the seat of our jeans, Kate. We'll just have to take it as it comes. I'll relieve you at Needles and we'll fuel and feed at Barstow."

"Let's hope nothing happens. I've had enough excitement for one day."

"That's a big ten-four," Barry said with a grin.

Kate groaned. "Jesus, Barry!"

Nothing did happen. The hot dusty miles peeled off behind them, as monotonous as the landscape that greeted them on both sides of the highway. At Needles, Kate swung the rig onto Interstate 40 and barreled west, the outline of the Sacramento Mountains to the south, the Providence Mountains to their northwest. They passed the Providence and stayed south of the Devil's Playground, rolling through the Bristol Mountains. They drove through the southernmost tip of Dry Troy Lake and pulled into a truck stop. Night was not far off.

"Eat and sleep?" Kate asked.

"In that order."

Later, snuggling close in the big sleeper, Kate's nakedness pushing softly against him, their hearts slowly calming after passion had cooled and softened, Kate sighed, her breath warm on Barry's neck, and said, "I've seen a lot of fights on the road, Barry. Rough-and-tumble fistfights between drivers. I've seen guys get their teeth knocked out and their jaws busted and their nose flattened. I've seen, oh, I don't know how many real bad wrecks, with people killed. But . . ."

She trailed it off and Barry picked it up, knowing what she was thinking. "But you've never seen anything like what went down this morning, right?"

"Yeah. Sorry I got sick."

"Don't be. It's natural."

"I mean . . . I didn't even think about it when I shot that guy. I just lifted the shotgun and pulled the trigger. Now, I feel . . ." She struggled inwardly for a word. "Well . . . *different*. You know what I mean?"

"Yes. I do."

"Did you get sick the first time you killed anybody?"

That flung Barry back twenty-five years. Back to the mean streets of New Orleans. Back when a street gang had confronted a fifteen-year-old boy and demanded his money. With about a dollar and a half in his jeans, Barry had decided it wasn't worth fighting over. He handed over his money. Then the leader of the gang shoved Barry back into the darkness of an alley, unzipped his pants, and told Barry to get on his knees and suck his cock.

Barry had told him, in graphic, four-letter words, what he thought of that idea. The other gang members, four of them, had moved toward Barry, grinning and balling their hands into fists.

The gang was streetwise, no doubt about that. They had hustled and mugged and robbed and raped and possibly killed to stay alive in their self-imposed cruel little world.

But Barry had been raised in the cab of a long-haul truck, back when trucking was a hell of a lot rougher than it is now. As a boy, he had lived through the union fights, the power struggles that left the offices and hit the highways. There was not much he had not seen.

Barry dropped to the dirty alley and rolled, picking up a broken wine bottle. He jammed the jagged end of the bottle into the exposed crotch of the gang leader. The young man dropped to the alley, screaming and bleeding from the puncture wounds. Rolling, coming to his feet, Barry jammed the broken bottle into a young man's face, driving one long shard of glass into an eye. The street hustler howled as his blood spurted. Spinning, Barry shoved the splintered ends of glass, now dripping blood, into the throat of a young punk.

Those remaining street punks split, racing away in fear of this wild young man.

Barry had looked at what he had done, his eyes meeting the pain-filled eyes of the gang leader, still on the dirty alley, holding his bleeding privates. "Not near as tough as you thought you were, huh, asshole?" Barry said.

He walked away, tossing his wino-made weapon against a brick wall, shattering it, forever erasing any fringerprints.

The next day he read in the paper where one of the punks had died, bleeding to death from a slashed and punctured throat.

Barry told his father about it.

"How do you feel about what you done, son?" Big Joe asked.

Barry shrugged. "They started it. I don't think I feel anything, Pop."

The father looked long into the son's eyes. "I know what you mean, boy. I was younger than you when I killed my first man. He was a bum. I was walkin' with your momma out near the Pontchartrain. We was just kids, holdin' hands and walkin'. He come up and told me what he was gonna do to your momma. Ugly, nasty things. I killed him with a knife. I didn't feel nothin'. You don't feel bad when you kill a rabid dog.'' His dad had shrugged. ''You, Barry, of my kids, you got my temper and disposition. You always gonna have to watch it. Now sit down and hear me good.

''Sometimes a person has to do what he has to do to survive. Before I'd see my momma or daddy or my wife or kids starve to death, I'd steal. But that would be if there was no work, nowhere. No little piece of ground to raise me a garden. No fish to catch. No game to hunt. And it just ain't that way, boy. It may be human nature to not be content with what a person has; but that don't give no one the right to steal if they's work to be had.

''To a very large point, boy, *everyone* has something to say about their destiny. I'm worth a lot of money, boy. But when I was your age, I didn't have a penny. Can you believe that, boy? Not a *penny*. But I never stole nothin' in my life. I never mugged nobody, never vandalized nobody's property. Everything I got, I worked for. And not no eight hours a day and quit, neither. If I thought *je* desire . . . I worked for it. I never axed nobody to *donnez-moi* nothin'.

''I got nothin' but *mepris* for criminals.'' He feigned a spit on the floor. ''They want it all but they don't wanna work for none of it. And then they gonna complain that they couldn't help themselves. Shit! Oh, they can help it, boy. If there ain't no work here, then go to Baton Rouge. No work there, go to Lafayette. A man ain't got an education . . . then get one. Got to the public library and check out books and *read*. Now, I butcher the English, boy. No doubt about it. But I ain't stupid. I talk the way I talk because I'm comfortable with it. But I can discuss economics, I can talk about the classics with some degree of expertise." He grinned. "Ain't that a fancy word. But you know what I'm sayin', don't you?"

"Yeah, I know what you mean, Pop. You've really read all those books in the house?"

"Every one of them, boy. Some of them, oh, maybe a dozen times."

He pointed out to Barry his favorite books, and Barry remembered that some of them had looked pretty damned dull at the time.

But in time he'd read and reread them all.

Kate brought him back to reality with a poke in the ribs. "I think I've lost you somewhere down the line, boy."

"Yeah. I was lost back in time. To answer your question . . . No, I didn't get sick the first time I killed a man. I was fifteen." He told her what had happened and about his conversation with his father afterward.

"Yeah. I know. Big Joe turned me on to books, too. Fifteen years old? Did you kill in Vietnam? Stupid question, I guess."

Did I kill in Vietnam? Barry thought. Oh, yes, Kate. But how to explain that to a civilian? You were about eight or nine when I went to 'Nam. Do you want me to tell you how it is to loop a garrote around a man's neck and choke him to death—silently, if at all possible, for you are behind enemy lines—if you could figure out where the damned lines were in 'Nam, that is. Or how about putting the knife blade in just the right spot to ensure almost instant death? That's good fun. Especially when your hand is over their mouth and they puke on you. Or bite you, as so often happens. Or set up swing traps, and then lie in ambush and listen to those impaled scream until they die? That's delightful. Or how about a good clean long-distance sniper shot? People ask, "Well, how do you know if you got a good hit from that distance."

"They fall funny," you reply.

And then the nosy questioner looks at you like you've just grown horns and a tail.

"Yeah. I killed in 'Nam, Kate."

"Does it bother you to talk about it?"

"Not really. But I seldom do."

"I don't understand you, Barry Rivers."

"Yeah? That's what my ex-wife used to say."

He felt her stiffen in his arms. "Well, that's what I really want to do, Barry. Talk about your goddamn ex-wife."

She rolled away from him . . . and fell out of the bunk. The things she said!

14

They ate a leisurely breakfast before dawn and pulled out, Barry taking the wheel for the first trick. About twenty miles outside of Bakersfield, with Kate at the wheel, she cut off on State 46 and connected with Interstate 5 just east of Lost Hills. They rolled at a steady 55 mph, as ordered. Nothing unusual happened; no one shot at them, attempted to force them off the road, gave them the bird ... nothing. Four hundred and fifty miles out of Barstow, they spotted a nice motel and pulled off the interstate. They were under government orders to travel no more than five hundred miles in a ten-hour period. With two drivers, that didn't make much sense to them, but when you work for the man, you obey his rules.

After a shower, Barry stretched out on the bed and called his attorney in Washington. "No way anyone could have known where we were going to stop, Ralph, so this phone is clear. How are things?"

"Everything appears normal on the surface," Ralph said. "But I'm getting whispers of tension among certain agencies. Man,"—he lowered his voice—"you and your people played hell in that shootout."

So much for keeping a lid on things. "Is it going to make the press?"

"Very doubtful. Oh, there might be a mention; but without names."

Then Barry dropped it all in Ralph's lap. He talked for a full five minutes, knowing Ralph was probably taping it all. When he finished, Ralph was silent for a full ten-count.

"A lawyer who is speechless?" Barry said. "I can't believe it. You're a disgrace to your profession."

"Jumping Jesus Christ, Barry!" the attorney finally blurted. "I had a hunch this thing might be big, but not that big."

"I have no proof, remember?"

"No, but you've convinced me. So it's dope that's behind it?"

"Maybe. And maybe the dope angle is just something to cover up something bigger."

Ralph groaned. "It's already complicated enough, friend. I'll go with the dope angle. What's your angle?"

"I don't know. Yet. The one thing I do know is that I'm being set up. For what? I don't know. Why? I don't know." He was conscious of Kate walking naked out of the bathroom; his eyes followed her.

She looked at him; her eyes drifted over his body. "Down, boy," she whispered. "First we eat."

Barry smiled.

"What do you want me to do on this end, Barry?" Ralph asked.

"Stay alert and be careful. Linda might suspect you're in this with me."

"Hell, I am! Now. Thanks to you."

"Stay loose, Ralph. I gotta go. I got a date with a blonde."

"I hope her name isn't Roy." He hung up.

Barry laughed and hung up. He looked at Kate. "Is your name Roy?"

She narrowed her eyes. "Boy, I worry about you at times. I really do."

The bad thing about it, Barry thought as he shaved the next morning, is that I really have no one to call if I get in trouble. With the exception of Ralph, I just don't know who to trust. I believe I can trust Fabrello, but I don't want heavy mob connections. Bad enough the mob is protecting Big Joe. Any more connections and . . .

He paused in wiping the lather off his face. Sure. She *wants* me to be caught playing footsie with Fabrello. God, I must be getting senile.

He walked to the phone and called New Orleans. Fabrello answered the phone. "No names," Barry said. "You know who this is?"

"I recognize the voice. Christ, what goddamned time is it? It's fucking dark outside."

"Seven o'clock, your time. Open the drapes. Is your phone secure?"

"Shit, no! Are you kidding? Every phone I got is bugged. We got rapists and robbers and muggers and perverts and assholes standing on every street corner of every city in America and the FBI is spending money bugging *my* phones. There ain't no justice in the world, pal. So what's on your mind at this godforsaken hour? And you got about thirty seconds to tell me before the phone cops start tracing your call."

"You're hot and I'm getting warmer. Our friend wants me as hot as you."

"Yeah. I figured that out. But we got a problem, you know?"

"Can you arrange independent security for the old trucker?"

"Can do and will. See you, boy."

Fabrello hung up. Barry looked at Kate, lying in the bed, looking at him.

"Get up, little one. It's time to get cracking."

They took their time driving the remaining one-hundred-and-fifty-odd miles to the cutoff point, enjoying the scenery as they trucked empty, northbound on Interstate 5. About thirty miles south of Redding, Kate at the wheel, they cut due west on a state highway.

"I don't know what in the hell is supposed to be down this way," Kate bitched. "Nothing shows on the map. Can you pick up anything?"

"Nothing shows between the interstate and the middle fork of the Cottonwood River. Our directions were precise. Did you check your odometer?"

"I didn't just fall off the turnip truck, Barry," she said dryly.

Barry laughed at her.

Exactly 28.7 miles later, they stopped half on the shoulder and half on the road and looked around them.

Nothing.

"Maybe the odometer is off a point," Barry suggested. "I'll climb down and walk up the road for a little bit."

"You be careful," Kate told him.

Barry tucked his 9mm behind his belt. "Bet on it, love."

About fifty meters later, Barry found the road, cutting

off to the north. He waved Kate forward and pointed her into the narrow road. He climbed back in, and within seconds the deep timber had swallowed them, truck and all.

"I hope this is the right road," Kate said. "I'd hate to have to back out of this mess."

They reached a closed gate with a small guardhouse behind the heavy chain-link fence. A man stepped out of the blockhouse and waved for them both to climb down.

The man, armed with a pistol and M-16, stayed behind the fence. "Shove your orders through the slot," he said.

Barry handed him the sealed orders. The guard opened the envelope, scanned the orders, and then nodded his head.

"Sorry for the cloak-and-dagger bit, driver. But this is a high-security area. Get back in your rig. When I open the gates, get through and do not, under any circumstances, stop your rig or get out until you reach the main post. Do not stop for *anyone;* do not pick up *anyone.* Do not get out of your rig until you are ordered to do so by a Mr. Carter. Do you both understand?"

"I understand."

The gate slid back on electrically controlled wheels. The guard waved them through, the gate closing behind them.

"What is this place?" Kate asked.

"Beats the hell out of me."

They almost ran into the main building. There were several buildings, all single-story and all so well camouflaged one could not see them until almost on top of them. Or, in this case, almost running into them. Barry knew they would be invisible from the air.

They sat in the truck for several minutes, both of them watching the door. It finally opened and a man in a white coat stepped out. He waved them out of the truck.

"My name is Carter. Let me see your orders." He quickly read the orders and handed them back to Barry, after tearing off his copy. He lifted his eyes to Barry. "How long has your refrigeration unit been running?"

"Since yesterday. About noon, I'd guess."

"You'd *guess?*"

Barry had taken an instant dislike for the man. "That's what I said."

"It's set at freezing, I hope."

"It's a mid-temp reefer, mister," Kate said. "It's not a Super Seal."

"I do not understand truck-driver jargon," Carter said. "What does that gibberish mean, woman?"

Kate stuck out her chin, her temper rising. "It means that this particular reefer is forty-two feet long and thirteen feet high. The interior lining is one-quarter-inch plywood with fiberglass. The capacity is about twenty-five hundred cubic feet. Steel cross-sills over critical areas—like the tandem and landing gear. The rear doors have single compression seals and one vent. The floor is one-and-a-quarter-inch aluminum extruded duct. The trailer supports are two-speed with roadside crank, sand shoes, and—"

"That will be quite enough," Carter said, waving her silent. "For God's sake, I am not in the least interested in any of that mess you just spouted. Be silent." He looked at Barry. "What is the lowest temperature you can maintain, driver?"

"About thirty-five degrees."

Kate was silent all right. Silently fuming.

"Goddammit!" Carter cussed. He shook his head and said, "It's not your fault, Rivers. You're just doing what you're told to do. Back your trailer up right there." He pointed. "Stop at the last door. Then you and Miss . . . ah, whatever her name is, go over there." Again he pointed.

"To that building. And wait in the lounge. Have some coffee. Some food if you like. Do not, repeat, *do not,* under any circumstances, come outside until you are told to come outside. Do you understand that?"

Barry resisted an impulse to tell the overbearing bastard where to shove his orders. "Yes, sir," he said.

"Fine. Now back your rig up."

Kate stood, watching Barry back the trailer, with Carter scurrying alongside, giving orders, which Barry promptly ignored.

Barry climbed down and Carter rushed up to him.

"You and your lady friend go to the lounge," Carter said. "Immediately!"

Walking toward the appointed building, Kate said, "I'd like to jerk a knot in that little man's ass!"

"Steady now, Kate, my dear."

"Screw you, Barry, my dear!"

The lounge was empty. Barry drew two cups of coffee from a drink machine and punched out two packages of sweet rolls. He and Kate took a table by a closed and draped window. Kate gently opened one drape and peeked outside.

"See anything interesting?" Barry asked.

"Not much." She eyeballed the outside. "Just some people putting boxes of stuff into a shipping container. Lifting it up with a forklift. What are those guys doing now?"

"I have no idea, Kate. What does it look like to you?"

"Looks like those bags they used in Vietnam."

That got his attention. He leaned over and peeked out through the tiny opening. He felt his stomach roll over. He quietly cursed.

"What's the matter, Barry?"

"Those are body bags, Kate. And they've got bodies in them."

15

Very little else was said between Kate and Barry until they had received their traveling orders, seen the doors sealed, and were on the road.

"This makes me feel creepy," Kate finally spoke. "God, Barry! Do those bags really have *bodies* in them?"

"I don't know. Looked like it. All right, we're Minnesota-bound, so call out the route."

"Don't we first go to Utah to meet the others?"

"Where we go is a quiet spot, far away from this . . . place, and pop that seal."

"Barry . . ."

"No way, Kate. I want to see what's in those body bags. If you don't want to be a part of it, I'll put you on a plane in Sacramento and you can fly back to New Orleans."

"Do you know what you can do with that suggestion?"

"I have a pretty good idea."

"Fine. So we backtrack and pick up Interstate 80 east.

If you've just got to pop that seal, we'll find a place." She shuddered. "I feel like I'm part of a horror movie."

"We may be," Barry agreed.

It was late afternoon when they hit the bypass around Sacramento and full night when they reached the deep timber of eastern California. Both knew from the way the rig handled they were not carrying much weight.

"How much does twenty-five or so bodies weigh?" Kate asked. "I sure would like to know what's in those other boxes."

"We'll find out. I didn't see anything other than the body bags. What did the boxes look like?"

"Kind of square. Looked heavy. And I saw them bringing in bags of ice."

Barry didn't even like to think what might be contained in the boxes. He forced his imagination to stop conjuring up ghoulish images.

They drove as far as their orders permitted. That put them in the Reno/Sparks area. They fueled, ate, and slept for six hours, pulling out at four the next morning. By daybreak they were some fifty-odd miles southwest of Winnemucca. Kate swung off on a state road and drove for a few miles, pulling off onto a dirt road and stopping.

"Let's try it here," she suggested.

They climbed down and stretched, breathing deeply of the clean, cool air. They walked around to get the kinks out of their muscles, then Kate got a punch set and began knocking out a new seal, one number at a time.

Barry walked to the rear of the reefer and popped the seal. He looked at Kate. "You ready for this?"

"You're the boss, boss."

He swung open the doors. The cold air hit them both, carrying with it the sickly sweet odor of death.

No dignity here, Barry thought, looking at the strapped-down body bags. He swung up and stepped inside the trailer, walking to a body bag. He looked at the tag.

CHESSMAN DONALD R. USMC. A service number followed, then a date and time. Barry had to assume that was the time and date of death. But how did he die? He mentally steeled himself, then slowly unzipped the bag. Death's odor struck him hard. Barry forced himself to look at the man's face. Chessman was about forty, he guessed. But what held his gaze was the scar that ran all around the man's head, the incision just above the eyes, and very crudely stitched.

Barry didn't like to think—No! The doctors wouldn't have removed his—

He shook that away and opened another bag. Another man about forty. Same hideous scar running all around the head.

"What is it, Barry?"

"You'd better see this, Kate. But brace yourself. It isn't pretty."

"I don't wanna look."

"Then don't."

She cussed, then climbed into the coldness of the reefer. She walked up to the first open bag, looked in, then ran to the rear and threw up. "Damn, Barry. That looks like something out of a Frankenstein movie." She wiped her mouth, coughed, and returned to Barry's side.

She followed him from bag to bag, gagging as he opened them one by one, and looking inside.

"Wanna make a bet as to what's inside those ice chests, Kate?"

"What do you mean?"

"You're looking at, I'd bet, what's left of experiments. And I'll make a bet that compound back in California houses an asylum. That's why the guy at the gate warned us not to stop or pick up anybody. All these men are servicemen, and I'll bet they're Vietnam vets. No families to care for them; or families who don't give a shit. No one is going to miss them. Human guinea pigs, Kate. Post Vietnam Syndrome. I'd bet a thousand bucks on that. It's a big issue now."

"That scar, Barry." She pointed. "They all have the same scar. What's that mean?"

"That's what's in those ice chests, Kate. How many chests did you see?"

"Oh, I don't know. Twenty, twenty-five, I guess."

"We're hauling twenty-five bodies. One ice chest to a body."

"What's in the chests?"

"One brain to a chest. These men have had their brains removed for study."

Kate passed out.

"Oh, Christ!" Kate said, sitting up on the bunk. "Where are we?"

"Coming up to Winnemucca. I put you in the sleeper and let you sleep. How do you feel?"

"Do you have to ask?"

She slid into the seat beside him and rubbed her face.

"Barry? Is what we're haulin' legal?"

"I seriously doubt it. Bill of lading says we're pulling delicate equipment for NASA. That answer your question?"

"Then . . . ?"

He shrugged. "That place wasn't just built, Kate. It's

been there for several years. So this has been going on for
a while."

"And you're planning on doing what?"

"I don't know. I don't know what I can do."

The officer who met them at the highly secret testing
facility in Utah told them the others had been sent south,
to Arizona. Some sort of hurry-up trip. They would all meet
back in New Orleans to await orders for their next trip.
Barry and Kate were to take the load on to Minnesota.

Barry nodded his understanding and walked back to his
rig, pointing the nose of the Kenworth straight north.

Back on the road, after a time of silence, during which
Kate studied his angry face, she said, "Kinda going the
wrong way to get to Minnesota, aren't we?"

"We'll get there."

"Uh-huh."

"I'm not going to follow the preplanned route, Kate."

"I sorta had that figured out. For a government project,
with SSTs, this thing seems kind of thrown-together to
me."

Barry was again silent for a time, thinking hard. Finally
he said, "Linda somehow found out about the experiment
station. I'll call it that for want of its proper name. She
was already working on the cocaine angle. She'd done a
lot of work setting up Fabrello and Bulgari." He shook his
head. "It seems to be all connected, but I can't find a way
to tie it all together."

"I'll tell you one thing. If we have to go back to that
place, I'd bet that's where they're doing whatever you have
to do with nose candy. Process it, maybe."

"That might be where the stuff is cut. But it's processed
out of the country. Yeah. You might have hit on it. But I

still can't tie it all together." He jerked his thumb toward the sleeper. "In my bag, Kate, there's a roll of film I took of the bodies while you were out. I've got to get it to my attorney in D.C."

"That Ralph fellow you were talkin' to the other night?"

"Yes. This thing is so confused and twisted. When I got into it, I thought I was fighting the mob. Now I firmly believe that Fabrello is being used, manipulated—like somebody, and I'm not even sure it's Linda, is attempting to do to me. I think Bulgari is a vain, silly, selfish person; for sure, he's being used. By Linda? Maybe. It points that way. But I can't be sure. Maybe *she's* being used by someone. Who? I don't know. Maybe Fabrello was wrong in his assessment of what's happening. Goddammit, Kate, I can't find the bottom line."

He cut his eyes to his left-side mirror. That car was still hanging back behind them. It had been there for some time, and it was beginning to annoy him.

"Does that look like a cop back there to you?" he asked.

"I been watchin' it. I don't know, Barry. No. Look hard. Four guys in that car. See them?"

"Yeah."

They were heading straight north, Salt Lake City just behind them. Barry planned to stay on Interstate 15 until they reached Butte, then cut straight east on 90, finally picking up Interstate 94, taking that into Minnesota.

"You plannin' on goin' into the high country, Barry?" Kate asked.

"Yeah."

"You ever driven it?"

"Nope."

"Stay on the interstate and it isn't bad. You get on those two-lanes, boy, it can get some kind of hairy up in the mountains."

"I've driven the Smokies a couple of times."

"The Rockies make the Smokies look like pimples. Believe it. That car's about to make a move, Barry."

"I can't believe they're going to try anything. It's too populated here."

The car accelerated past them.

"Hard-lookin' ol' boys," Kate observed.

"M-16 laying on the floorboards of the back seat," Barry told her. "Or an AR-15. I couldn't quite tell."

"That lets out a bunch of businessmen, don't it?"

Barry watched the car pull back into the right lane. He checked his mirrors. Another car had pulled in behind them.

Four men sitting in it.

"Yeah," he said softly, just loud enough for her to hear. "Unless their business is murder."

16

"Barry," Kate said, looking at him. "If we are carryin' dope, we're gonna deliver it. Why would anyone risk bringin' the government down on them by attackin' an SST when the dope is gonna be delivered anyway?"

"I can't answer that, Kate. This whole thing is crazy. Look at that sky. We're about to hit some crappy weather."

The sky had abruptly darkened; this close to dusk, night suddenly settled her skirts over the land. The first fat drops of rain splattered on the windshield. Barry cut on his lights and wipers. The car that had passed them now had slowed, staying just ahead of the eighteen-wheeler. The second car was staying behind them.

"Surely they don't think they're going to box us in with any degree of success?" Barry said aloud.

"You'd be surprised, or maybe you wouldn't, what a lot of four-wheelers think, Barry."

Barry signaled and swung out into the left lane. The car

behind him stayed in the right lane. "If I knew for sure that guy was going to pull something, I'd slap his ass off the side."

"You can't be sure of that!" Kate said, just a bit too swiftly for Barry's liking.

His eyes narrowed, but he kept his mouth shut. *Kate?* No . . . that didn't make sense. But hell, he thought, what *has* made any sense so far?

"I didn't mean for it to sound like that, Barry," she said. "A load of dead bodies is not worth killing some innocent people."

"Sure. Forget it, Kate. I'm going to shake one of these cars. How far to the 84 loop back to 80 east?"

She looked at her truckers' atlas. " 'Bout ten miles. Get off on 89 right up here. It's thirty-one miles to 80. But then what?"

Barry risked a glance at the atlas. "We give them their chance in Wyoming. You game?"

"You're drivin'," she said flatly. Too flatly. "Where in Wyoming?"

"We'll take 189 north."

"I run it a couple of times. It's a damn good place for an ambush. I run up to Jackson half a dozen times. It's a son of a bitch in the winter."

Barry took a chance. "What's on your mind, Kate?"

She shook her head.

"Come on, Kate. You're going to make me paranoid and I won't be able to trust you."

"Barry, Big Joe is all right. You put the fire back under his butt and steel in his backbone. Nobody is gonna take his line from him. Right?"

"Yeah. So?"

"You could stop right now, and your lady friend up in Washington couldn't do a damn thing to you. Right?"

"That's correct. I suppose. What are you getting at, Kate?"

"What's the government payin' you to risk your ass, Barry?"

"Nothing. You know that."

"You're a millionaire arms dealer, ain't you, Barry?" she asked softly, as softly as the rumble and roar of an eighteen-wheeler would allow, that is.

"Yes. I've hinted at that to you. It shouldn't come as any surprise."

"A millionaire. Yet you're assin' around with a poor truck-driver lady. Why, Barry?"

Barry smiled. He got it then. "Y'all think I'm a-triflin' with yore affections, ma'am?" he drawled.

"How would you like to get slapped, boy?"

"You'll wreck us both, girl."

"Barry, don't you know of *anybody* up there in Washington you could turn all this . . . mess over to? Let them handle it?"

Well, he halfway had it. She was worried about *him*.

Something very soft and gentle and somehow sad touched him inwardly. It had been a long time since he had felt anything like it. He looked at the blonde looking at him. There were tears in her eyes.

"I think I'll just keep you around, girl. Providing that's all right with you."

"I'll think about it some, boy. Let you know later on."

"Fine. Now listen for a minute. After we get on 80, you and I are going to change seats; but we're not going to stop rolling to do it. OK?"

"That's no problem. But why?"

"Because, Kate, my girl, you are a better driver than I am."

She busrt into tears.

"Now what did I do?" Barry asked.

"That's the nicest thing any man ever said to me, Barry Rivers!"

Barry threw back his head and roared with laughter. Yep—she was definitely a keeper.

The gentle shower turned into a full-blown storm, the rain lashing down in sometimes-near-blinding sheets. Barry slowed his speed and changed seats with Kate; not something he wanted to do again in a blinding rainstorm. Thirty minutes later she had exited off on Interstate 80 and was rolling east. The intersection with Highway 189 was about forty-five miles up the road.

They pulled over just inside Wyoming to weigh, but the scales were closed. Ten miles later, Kate swung the rig onto 189.

"This will be where they hit us, Barry. It's almost forty miles to the next town. And this road can get tight."

Barry busied himself checking first his Uzi, then Kate's shotgun. "Let them make the first move, Kate. Let's hope they hit us on a flat so you can swing into the left lane. If not, you're going to have to slap the car off the road. Can you do that?"

Her face tightened. "One time there was this ol' boy over in Alabama. He come up to me in a truck stop and wouldn't leave me alone. Said some pretty rough things to me. I made him mad and he come after me on the road. Started firin' at me; him and the ol' boy with him. I slapped that damned four-wheeler off the road and into the Tallapoosa River. Never did know what became of them."

Barry didn't doubt the story for a bit. "Check your mirrors, Kate."

"Two cars behind us. I can't tell if they're the same ones as before."

"We'll soon find out."

The rain had tapered off into no more than an annoying drizzle; that type of drizzle that kept a driver turning the wipers off and on—and kept a driver cussing.

Kate drove and Barry rode in silence. Kate concentrated on driving the slick highway, and Barry was still attempting to tie all the pieces of the complicated puzzle together. It came as no surprise to him when, after his ruminations, he was no closer to fully understanding what was going on.

With a sigh that Kate could hear he gave it up and brought all his attentions back to the present.

They were in the middle of a curve, blind front and back, when suddenly the lights of a car, on high-beam, came flashing around them.

"Crazy son of a bitch!" Kate yelled. "Jesus Christ!"

"That's them, Kate. They've started their move."

Bright sparks flashed in the night as the men in the back seat of the lead car began firing at the Kenworth. Slugs began whining off the cab.

"That's it!" Barry yelled. "Goddammit!" he roared. He lowered his window, leaned out, and gave the sedan a full clip from his Uzi.

The back window of the sedan exploded in a splintering shower of glass.

With the lights of the Kenworth on bright, both Barry and Kate could see the carnage the Uzi created in the sedan. They watched the blood splatter as the two men in the rear were thrown forward by the impacting slugs.

The rear end of the sedan slewed around as the driver fought to maintain control. He almost lost it, then corrected the slide and began slowing down, the sedan in the middle of the road, attempting to force the Kenworth to stop.

"Ram him!" Barry yelled.

Kate shifted and plowed into the rear of the car. Sparks flew as the rear tires of the sedan blew out and the frame and bumper began dragging the concrete. As they entered another curve, Kate let up on the pedal and the car broke free, sliding to the right. The sedan spun crazily in the road and then went over the side, busting through the guardrail, plunging downward into a ravine. Both Kate and Barry thought they could hear the screams of the men still inside the doomed vehicle.

The car turned end over end and was soon lost from sight in the misty night.

"One down," Barry muttered. "Now let's see what these other clowns want to do."

"Little Muddy bridge just up ahead," Kate informed him.

"Good a place as any," Barry replied, inserting a fresh clip into the belly of the Uzi.

"Barry? Why are they doing this to us?"

He was honest in his reply. "I don't know, Kate. But somehow, someway, I'm going to find out."

But it was not to be that night. When Kate again checked her mirrors, the second car had vanished, falling back into the misty night.

"Keep going," Barry told her. "But just to be on the safe side,"—he checked the atlas—"when we get up here to Diamondville, I think it is, take 30 back to the interstate. Just in case those in the second car call the state police. With any kind of luck, they'll think we're heading north, not east."

"You think they might do that?"

"They might. It'll be their word against ours, and you know how a lot of people feel about truckers."

"Tell me," she replied, with more than a touch of bitterness in her voice.

They stopped once for fuel and food and coffee, and once to weigh, before leaving Wyoming. They had rolled on through the night. Alternately driving and sleeping, violating all the rules of their government contract, they rolled on, always angling toward the north whenever they could, always on two-lane highways. They were on schedule when they pulled into northern Minnesota, but their logbook was a shambles. As it so often happens with longhaulers, neither one of them really knew what day it was.

Barry had remembered to express-mail the film to Ralph, with a brief note attached, telling him to be very careful with the film and that Barry would call him in a few days.

It came as no surprise to either of them to discover, upon reaching their drop-off point, that it was deep in the woods of a government-owned wildlife management area, and that the buildings were almost identical to those they had seen back in California.

It was the same procedure: the closed compound, the armed guards, the camouflaged buildings . . . and a smart-assed director.

"You're late," he said shortly, without introducing himself.

Both Barry and Kate were tired and gritty-eyed and grimy. And Barry was in no mood to take a lot of lip from some officious desk jockey.

"If you'll take a good look at the front of that truck, you might understand why we're late, Mister-Whoever-in-the-hell-you-are."

The white-coated man looked hard at Barry, then inspected the front of the Kenworth. He looked back to Barry. "Nebbling," he said. "These look like bullet holes."

"That's exactly what they are," Kate told him. "It's kind of hard to keep on schedule when people are shooting at you."

"Did any of them puncture the trailer?" Nebbling asked. Not, "Are either of you hurt?"

No instant camaraderie here, Barry thought. "No."

"Did you report the incident to the police?"

"No. We took an evasive route. That's why we're late." By about four hours, he thought.

"Good," Nebbling said, allowing himself a smile. "Very good. Very smart on your part. I congratulate you both. Tell me what you think the dollar amount of damage will be, and I'll give you the money. Cash."

Kate had walked to the rear of the reefer. She called, "You wanna inspect the cargo, mister?"

"No!" Nebbling cried. "Don't open those doors."

Kate walked around the rig, the broken seal in her hand. "Oh, I'm sorry. I popped the seal. I just figured you'd wanna check the cargo."

"Ah . . . no. We'll do that later. But thank you for your concern."

They received the same instructions as before. Back the rig up to the side of the building. Go get some coffee. Wait.

"Good thinking," Barry told Kate as they walked to the appointed building.

"I didn't want them lookin' too close at that homemade seal."

"You see the new trailer parked over there?"

"Yeah. And it's got some weight in it. See how those supports are diggin' in?"

"Yeah. Whatever it is, we're not hauling bodies this run."

"No," Kate agreed. "Maybe just a lot of pieces of bodies. Mixed in with a bunch of other gruesome stuff."

"Well, we'll know when we get our orders."

When he received his orders, his smile was very thin.

"Where we takin' this load, Barry?" Kate asked.

"Maine. Way up in the northern part."

"Where not very many people live, right?"

"Yeah."

"Like I said, Barry. Pieces of bodies and other gruesome stuff."

17

Barry got the impression that Mr. Nebbling thought he was just another truck driver—ignorant to the core. He knew that many people thought that. And he knew that many people were wrong. But if that's what Nebbling thought, fine.

"We were told we'd be headin' back south after this run, boss," Barry said. "Deadheadin'. Is there any great rush on this load?"

"Why do you ask?" Nebbling inquired, his eyes narrowing suspiciously.

" 'Cause me and the old lady would like to check into a motel and take a good bath, sleep in a real bed; maybe just for one night—if that's all right with you, that is."

"Oh. Well. No, I don't mind. I'm sure it must be . . . uncomfortable in one of those trucks. Besides, if you leave this instant, you'll get there on a Sunday. I don't want that.

Yes, spend a night resting. I'll make a notation in your orders."

That five-hundred-mile daily limit again.

"I'm sure looking forward to that motel room and a bubble bath, boy," Kate said.

Barry grinned as he headed south, toward Minneapolis/St. Paul. "Oh, you're gonna get that bubble bath, Kate. But it's gonna be a while yet."

She groaned. *"Now* what do you have up your sleeve?"

"We're going to, as my dad used to say, highball it, Kate. We're going to dodge the scales, get our logbook all screwed up, and maybe get put of the SST business. But we're going to be in Washington, D.C., thirty hours from now."

"That's no hill to climb," Kate said. "Just put the pedal to the metal and hammer down."

Stopping along the way, Barry called some friends in D.C. and pulled a few strings, managing to arrange storage of the SST at a military base. Under guard. He had called Ralph from a truck stop outside St. Cloud.

Yes, he had the prints. They made him ill. They were hideous. What the hell was going on?

That's what we're going to find out, Barry told him. Then he asked his friend to do a few more things.

Barry and Kate hit the interstate system and kept on trucking. As they rode and drove, Barry firmed up his plans. He was tired of it; tired of not knowing what was going on and who he could trust.

He outlined part of his plan to Kate.

"Isn't it a little soon to be goin' for the big enchilada?" she asked.

"Yes. Maybe too soon. But Ralph is arranging for the best PSE operator in the Washington area to be at my apartment. If Linda refuses to take the test, she's damning herself. I'm tired of not knowing who I can trust."

"I'm with you, Barry," she said.

"For better or worse?" he kidded her gently.

She grinned. "You said it, boy. Now I'm gonna hold you to it."

They shaved hours off Barry's projected time, averaging 60 mph, rolling night and day. They took a taxi from the base to Barry's apartment.

"Wow!" Kate said, looking around the luxury apartment. "This is beautiful. This yours?"

"I lease it, yes. One of the bathrooms is that way." He pointed. "Ralph was going to have someone electronically sweep this apartment." He looked at his writing desk in the den. His clock was moved to the other side of the desk, a signal that the apartment was clean. "It's been done. I'll start setting things up. We've got thirty-six hours to play with before we have to move."

"Bathtub, here I come!" Kate said.

Linda O'Day and Kate Sherman eyeballed each other. It was not what one would call a terribly friendly exchange of glances.

The PSE operator, a man who identified himself as Nesson, was setting up his equipment. John Weston, a senior inspector for the FBI who had been friends with Barry for years, was in attendance, sitting quietly in a chair in the den. Ralph Martin sat on the couch. A very nervous gentleman from the Treasury Department was standing by the wet bar. The man in charge of the Washington, D.C., area IOLDG, Walt, was sitting in a Boston rocker, a faint smile on his lips.

The Treasury man watched as Barry clicked on a reel-to-reel recorder. "This cannot," he said, "in any way be construed as a legal proceeding."

"You have something to hide, Jackson?" Walt asked him.

"I have nothing to hide," Jackson said stiffly.

"I don't like this a damn bit, Barry," Linda said. "I stuck my neck out for you and this is the way you're repaying it?"

"I want the truth," Barry replied. "Now everybody just sit tight and listen to me for a few minutes. I'm going to take it from the top and let the chips fall."

He began with his call to New Orleans—it seemed like months back, instead of only days—and took it step by step, day by day, event by event. When he spoke about his suspicions of Linda, he stared at her, never taking his eyes from her. And she met his gaze without flinching.

Barry was surprised when he had finished and glanced at the clock. He had talked for twenty minutes.

Barry sat down beside Kate and looked at John Weston. "Your turn, John."

The FBI inspector sighed. "I wish you had come to me in private with this, Barry. Now, if any of your suspicions are valid, I don't know what I can do about it."

"It wouldn't have made any difference," Linda said. "The results would have been the same."

"Would you care to elaborate on that?" Barry asked her.

"I underestimated you, Barry," Linda said. "I shouldn't

have done that. You'd make a damn fine investigator—if you'd quit playing with guns."

"Back to that," Barry replied.

"I don't like guns, Barry," Linda openly admitted. "I never have. I've always been open about that. But if you, any of you,"—her gaze swept the people in the den— "think I would turn sour and play footsie with the mob over a personal conviction of mine, then I feel . . . dirtied. And betrayed by the country I work for and the people who pay my salary."

John said, "Since it's doubtful any of this is going to leave this room, Linda, would you care to comment on your relationship with Bobby Bulgari?"

"I've been meeting with Bulgari for over a year. Slowly building a case on the southern mob. He doesn't know who I am."

"You're not serious?" Ralph said. "Of *course* the man knows who you are. The mob has more lawyers in this part of the country than the Justice Department has."

"Fabrello is convinced some people in very high places within the government are involved in the smuggling in and selling of dope," Barry said. "And I believe him."

"So do I," Linda said. "That's part of what I'm working on. But I am convinced that Bulgari doesn't know who I am. My cover was done by experts within the . . ."

She paused for a few seconds. A very thin smile parted her lips.

"By whom, Linda?" John asked.

"Experts within Justice, working with three FBI agents out of some southern office. *Shit!*" she blurted, disgust in her voice, as the realization that she had been had sank in.

Barry rose to his feet and paced the room for a moment.

He turned and faced the group. "Do any of you realize what I've accomplished this morning?"

They sat and looked at him, waiting.

"All I've succeeded in doing is making matters more complicated."

"For a lot of us," John said. "Hoover is spinning in his grave." He lifed his eyes to Linda. "I'm going to need the names of all who helped set up your cover."

"I'll sure give it to you," she said. Her eyes were blazing with an inner anger, scarcely concealed.

"I'd like to know who the men were who first approached my father about this SST business," Barry said.

"I can get that for you," John said.

Nesson had sat quietly, saying nothing, but his eyes had been, for several minutes, on the Treasury man. "You seem awfully nervous, Jackson. Is something the matter?"

Jackson sat down on a padded barstool. He rubbed his face with his hands. "Jesus Christ, people," he said. "You're all opening a fucking can of worms. And you haven't even gotten the lid off yet."

"And you're not talkin' about dope, either, are you, Jackson?" Kate spoke for the first time.

"You know something I need to know, Kate?" Barry asked her.

"I know I don't trust this slick dude," she said, pointing at Jackson.

"Well, you'd be wrong in assuming that, miss," Jackson said. "But correct in assuming my concern is not about dope."

"Well, *my* concern damn sure is!" Weston said.

"Ah, crap!" Jackson said. "You all-American types at the Bureau fry my butt! You people are so goddamned concerned about your precious image you'd wade through shit and swear it was roses."

"I agree," Nesson said. It was not the best-kept secret in the world that Nesson did a lot of work for the CIA. Very covert work.

"Who asked you?" John said.

Nesson laughed at him. He picked up the pictures Barry had taken and Ralph had developed. He looked at them, then held them out to Jackson. "This is what you're referring to, correct?"

"Yeah," the Treasury man muttered. "But it's out of our jurisdiction. So far, we can't come into the picture."

"Would somebody please tell me what is going on?" Kate asked.

"Perhaps you don't have a need to know," Linda said primly.

"Fuck you!" Kate told her.

"Now, ladies," Walt said.

"Go sit on a candlestick!" Linda told him.

"Knock it off!" Barry growled. "Goddammit, let's don't start yammering at each other." He looked at Jackson. "Dope is bad enough. And I'm convinced it's being hauled by SSTs. But not by my outfit. We were decoys, I'm thinking. Who tried to hijack us and why, Jackson? And what about those . . . *brains* we hauled out of California?"

Jackson looked at him. "It's the end of my career if any of this leaves this room."

"Looks to me," Kate said, her face still mirroring the horror of brainless bodies, "a lot of peoples' careers were ended at that . . . *place* out in California."

Jackson paced the den, alone with his silent thoughts. When he finally spoke, his voice was low-pitched. "I'm convinced the President doesn't know what is taking place at these facilities. But . . . someone, I don't know who, has apparently decided that since these men, these veterans, have all gone off the deep end, no longer functional human beings—crazies, someone referred to them—they could nevertheless make a contribution to the study of combat-related stress. There are, so I'm told, several of these . . . well, facilities in the United States. VA hospitals are becoming very crowded." He shrugged his shoulders.

"Where does the dope come into the picture?" Barry asked.

"A group of younger agents, looking for a way to make a fast buck, found out about the research. Since SSTs were carrying the . . . illegal research anyway, why not put three or four million dollars' worth of dope in with the bodies and brains and so forth." He looked at Weston. "Don't worry, John. It's not confined solely to your All-American bunch. Half a dozen agencies are involved."

"I think it's hideous," Weston replied. "Not just the dope, but the entire gruesome affair. How long have you known about this?"

"Oh . . . maybe ninety days. Since I don't know who to trust, I've had to work in silence."

"You intimated that you are not alone with this knowledge," Ralph said.

"You're right. I've talked with three close friends of mine within my agency. Borman, Jennings, Stemke. We've been working very quietly gathering information. It's been slow going. For obvious reasons . . ."

"Explain the obvious reasons," Barry said.

"The project—I don't know what it's called—is one reason, naturally. Obviously, it's going on with the blessings of someone in government. The dope angle, for another reason." He looked at Barry. "But don't think for an instant those behind all this don't know who you are, Rivers. For they do. I think that's probably the reason you were attacked."

"Possibly. But if that's true, then there are sure as hell more than three or four rogue agents involved."

"Looks that way, doesn't it?"

Nesson tapped his PSE machine. "I think we'd best get this over with, ladies and gentlemen."

Linda stood up and removed her jacket. "I want my name cleared. Let's do it."

18

The testing did not take as long as many people unfamiliar with psychological stress testing might think. And when it was concluded, all present had confirmed their innocence.

At least as far as the machine and its operator could take it.

More relaxed now, over fresh-brewed coffee, the group sat and began thrashing the chaff from the wheat.

"How about the pictures, John?"

The FBI man hesitated. "I don't think one person should have them all. I think they should be divided among us and more pictures made from the negatives."

"I agree," Jackson said. "Barry, what are you hauling this trip?"

"I don't know, for sure."

"Let me call Stemke," the Treasury man said. "He can look at that seal and make a new one. You said a while ago it was different from the last seal that Miss Sherman broke."

"That's true. But let's lay it all out first. Linda, you've got coworkers involved in this thing. You're going to have to be very careful."

She nodded in agreement. "You really don't believe Fabrello is involved in any of this, do you?"

"No, I don't. I can't tell you why I believed what he told me, but I did. And while I'm thinking about it, let me call him right now. I just remembered something."

He dialed the capo's number in New Orleans and got him on the line. "I'll keep it short. You know who this is. What about the keys in the trash can?"

Fabrello grunted. "I didn't know whether you was dead or alive. It's a whole new ballgame, boy. That car was bought by the government. You know what that means?"

"I sure do. Thanks."

Fabrello hung up.

Barry told the others what the Mafia capo had said.

"He didn't say what government agency it was assigned to, did he?" Jackson said.

"No."

Nesson looked at Linda. "Since I seem to be a part of this . . . well, operation, whether I wanted in or not, tell me this: Is there a chance this Bulgari might be the head of this particular snake?"

"I don't think so. Bobby is a very intelligent man. He's one of the new breed of hood. Educated at the best schools, speaks several languages. Understands business. But he's very vain and very greedy. All right, I'll admit I've been stupid about my role. I suppose Bobby does know who I am and he's been using me. So I get to toss my investigation reports in the garbage. But I don't believe he's the honcho of this operation."

"You'd best break off your association with Bulgari, Linda. Or you just might meet wtih a very tragic accident. And be careful doing it," John warned. "It's a cinch we've all got two or three or more coworkers involved in this matter."

Jackson stood up. "Let's check that load, Barry."

It was not a pretty sight.

Linda had returned to her office at Justice; Kate chose to stay at the apartment. Walt returned to his IOLDG offices. Barry, Ralph, Jackson, John, and Nesson rode out to the base. There they met with Stemke. The Treasury man looked at the seal, said it was a piece of cake, and popped it.

"This equipment is shit," John said. "It's just useless junk stored in containers for weight. Here's your real cargo."

Barry's usually strong stomach did a flip-flop. He fought back sickness, and, he was sure, the others were doing the same.

His cargo was various parts of human bodies, all carefully stored in some sort of liquid. And dead dogs and cats . . . at least pieces of the animals. Stored in the same liquid. And boxes of medical records and reports.

Barry disliked animal research; he disliked cruelty of any type to any animal. Even though he knew animal research was important, he didn't like it. And he especially did not like to see painful research done on dogs and cats . . . pets.

"Bastards!" Ralph said.

Barry did not know if the lawyer was referring to the animals or to the humans. Probably both.

"Crap like this makes me wonder what kind of country we're living in," Nesson said.

"I've wondered about that for years," John said, very much unlike the usually taciturn FBI agent he was.

"Do I deliver the load?" Barry asked.

"You'll have to," Jackson said. "Give us time to set things up. No pun intended," he said, smiling grimly.

"Do we search for dope?"

Both Treasury and FBI shook their heads. "Wouldn't do any good. This is an illegal search. If anyone came forward, we might even have to give the dope back to them," John added.

"Neither of you think I've been carrying any dope, do you?" Barry asked.

"I don't," Jackson said. "I think you're running a decoy. One of your other rigs is carrying the dope."

Barry looked at John. The FBI man nodded in agreement.

When Barry spoke, his tone was testy. "Is this it, then? Is this the bottom line I've been looking for? How does dope and government research tie in? Are we missing something? If so, what is it?"

"You sound like a cop now, Barry," John told him as they stood outside the rig, watching Stemke replace the seal.

"It bugs me," Barry admitted. "Why were we ambushed? To draw attention away from the rig that was really carrying the contraband? I could accept that if I just knew it was so."

"We'll know the answers to your questions when we break the case," Jackson said. "If," he added grimly, "we ever do."

Kate and Barry pulled out before dawn the next morning. They skirted Baltimore, picking up 695, slowly working their way toward what truckers call the Dirty Side—primarily New York and New Jersey. They rolled through the Pennsylvania countryside and into New York State, keeping well west of the Dirty Side.

There was no really easy or interstate-connected way, directly, to get to northern Maine. It was just a matter of slowly edging northeastward. Barry had called the terminal to check on the other drivers and to warn them to be careful; no one knew for sure what was going to happen.

The trip was uneventful, the weather beautiful, the highways dry and accident free. They rolled through New Hampshire and into Maine, connected with Interstate 95, and stayed with it until reaching northern Maine; then they cut off on Highway 11, but not before fueling the Kenworth and feeding themselves.

"You ever pulled up in here?" Barry asked Kate.

"Not this far," she admitted, while consulting a map. "Damn sure isn't much up this way, is there?"

"Perfect spot for what our government is doing to our veterans."

"I heard that."

It was a replay of California and Minnesota: same desolate area, heavily barricaded and guarded compound, same low block buildings, same warnings from the gate guard about not stopping or picking up anybody.

"Yeah," Barry said. "We've heard it all before."

"It don't hurt to refresh your memory," the gate guard said. "We've got some real psychos in here, man."

The first crack in their secrecy, Barry thought. Someone finally admitted something.

"Oh, yeah?" Barry said, without much enthusiasm. "Well, I hope you got the crazies locked down good."

"Oh, they get out every now and then," the gate guard admitted.

"Well, I hope you're carryin' live ammo."

"Believe it. I busted a cap on one two, three months ago," the guard said proudly.

"Kill him?"

"Deader than hell."

"Good. I got enough to worry about without having to worry about some criminal jumpin' out of the bushes at me."

"Oh, they're not criminals. Not really. They're just nuts, man. Vets from 'Nam that went off their nut, you know?"

"Yeah, I know." Barry looked at the guard, pegging him as being far too young to have served in 'Nam. "Stupid fuckin' war," he said.

"Wasn't it? I don't have no sympathy for these suckers we got locked down in here. Shell-shocked, or something like that, they claim. Ask me, they was crazy 'fore they went over there. What's the big deal about shootin' some gooks and slopes? Huh?"

"Yeah. No big deal." The guy wanted to talk, so Barry let him.

"It'll be a few more minutes, driver." He looked at Kate, sitting in the cab. "Your wife?"

"Codriver."

The guard smiled. "That must get cozy at times, huh?"

"Sure does," Barry said, winking at the asshole. "Must get lonesome around this place for you?"

"Huh?"

"No women."

"Oh, we got women locked down inside. Some of them damn good-lookin'. They'll put some of that pussy on you for cigarettes and stuff like that, you know?"

"Yeah. I know. And they ain't gonna raise any hell about being raped, right?"

"Shit, no! They're so popped up most of the time they don't know what's going on."

"Yeah, so I heard. We just pulled a load from the West Coast. Talked to some guys out there."

"They gettin' some of that inmate stuff strapped on them, too, huh?"

"Hell, yes!"

The guard laughed. "Well, hell, it ain't so bad for them. They got all the free dope they want. For as long as they last, that is."

"I know what you mean." Free dope? "I guess it's better to test on humans than animals?"

"You got that right, buddy. Sometimes the doctors pop 'em too hard, though; too much shit. They just wander off and drop dead."

"That's what we're haulin' this run," Barry told him. "Bits and pieces, you know?"

The guard shuddered. "Yeah, I know. That's what you'll probaby be haulin' out of here, too. One of these days, the doctors will find out what they're looking for, I suppose."

"Yeah. And then we'll both be out of a job."

"Huh? Naw! I've worked all over the country in these places. California, Utah, Georgia, Texas—must be thirty, forty of these places. Well, maybe not that many. You'd know more about that than me."

"Not that many."

The guard laughed. "Just checkin' you, buddy. Don't take it the wrong way. Twelve of them. Who'd ever think the government would be in the dope business, huh?"

"Yeah."

"You ever hauled any live ones, yet?"

"Once," Barry lied, not really knowing what the guard was talking about, but having a sick feeling he just might know.

The guard confirmed it. "Ain't that a real pisser, man? Did you haul shell-shocked nuts or greasers?"

"Aliens."

"Yeah. Right. Aliens." He grinned. "Shit! The Mexicans don't know how many people they got down there anyway. They ain't gonna miss three, four hundred a year no way."

"You're right. But I'll tell you what pisses me off. It's the guys who round up the greaseballs for us that are makin' all the good bread."

"Man, you are so right. I tried to get in on that end of it. I got my hands slapped real quick and hard."

"You're not alone, buddy," Barry told him in a low voice. "I damn near lost my job."

"No kidding?"

"Yeah. It just so happened the head knocker of the whole operation picked that time to come south. I damn near got seriously dead."

The guard chuckled. "Yeah? I bet Mr. Morris was kinda pissed."

Barry felt a sudden sickness in his stomach. "You're sure right. Little Fatty Jack was some kind of pissed."

"Fatty Jack! That's a good one. Bet you never called him that to his face, though?"

"No. Hell, no. But Mr. Morris was some kind of hot about it. Fat-ass bastard chewed me out. I could have broke him in half. Then he sticks the money in his pocket and goes back home. Somewhere down south, I think."

"Maryland. He's some kind of a weapons expert for the government." The guard looked toward the compound. "They're motioning for you to come on, buddy. Nice talkin' to you. Maybe I'll see you next trip."

"Yeah. Maybe. Good talkin' to you, too, buddy." Real good, *buddy*. Just great.

19

"We're haulin' the same kind of stuff, Barry?" Kate asked. "You sure?"

"That's what the guard told me." He swung the rig out of the compound and onto the state road. Among other things, he thought.

"Where to?"

"Our orders say to Georgia, but we're stopping in Washington. I've had enough of this shit, Kate. I'm packing it in and turning it over to the federal boys."

He was silent until reaching Highway 11. He leveled with her, telling her everything the guard had said.

Then it was Kate's turn to be silent. With silent tears running down her face.

"All right, Kate. I get the feeling those tears aren't for the poor vets and the Mexicans. You want to level with me?"

She wiped her face and said, "I've heard talk about this,

Barry. Not on the CB. But just gossip. Sittin' around the truck stops late at night."

"And you and the others did . . . what about it?"

"Barry, there was no proof it was really happening. By the time you get to the next truck stop, or you drop your load, you've forgotten all about it."

"You're lying to me, Kate."

"Yeah? Maybe I am. Look, Barry, you know as well as I do that ninety-nine percent of the drivers out here wouldn't put up with no haulin' human cargo."

"Make it about eighty-five percent, Kate, and maybe I'll go along with that figure. The rest are redneck, asshole, dipshit types and *you* know *that.*"

"Oh, yeah?" She stared out the window. "Well, maybe you're right."

Drop it, Barry, he thought. You've forgotten the silent Code of the Road.

"95 will take us straight into D.C.," Kate said. "It's a pretty easy run." She glanced at him. "Mad at me?"

"Not really. I guess I'm sort of down about the whole slimy matter."

"Maybe you're glad it's just about over?"

"Could be."

Neither of them could know it was just beginning for one of them.

And very near the end for the other.

"What happens now, Barry? To us?"

"If you're agreeable, I hang up my truck-driving boots and we head back to Maryland."

"We?"

"We."

"How about your partner? This Jack Morris?"

"I don't know if the law can do anything to Jack. But I can, if they fail. Whatever, the partnership is dissolved."

"No doubt in your mind it's him?"

"No. There is only one Jack Morris that is an arms expert. Believe me, I know them all."

"You think I can fit in your world, Barry?" There was a sadness in her voice.

"Yes. Don't you?"

"I don't know. I don't have much experience with fancy people."

He smiled. "You'll do just fine, Kate. Trust me."

"Can you move on this information?" Barry asked Weston and Jackson.

Treasury and FBI looked at one another. John said, "No. But we can get the ball rolling."

"And what does that mean?"

"I mean it's a beginning, Barry," Jackson told him.

"Crap! What it means is you've got to take it before grand juries and all that horseshit. By the time you get around to raiding those . . . hellholes, you'll find nothing."

"We've got to do it the legal way, Barry."

"I don't," Barry said tightly. "By God, I don't have to."

"Take it easy, Barry," Ralph cautioned him.

Take it easy? By the time the wheels of so-called justice get spinning, a lot of innocent men and women will be doped up, cut up, and disposed of. And you're telling me to take it easy?"

"Barry, it's the way the system works; has to work," Jackson said patiently. "Now that we know who the head man is, we'll stake him out, bug his phones, and start gathering information."

Kate snorted, very unladylike. All turned to look at her, sitting on the couch of Barry's apartment. "Why don't you guys just go in, jerk him up, kick his ass a time or two, and he'll start talkin' so fast you'll have to slow him down to keep up.''

"Then any information we obtained under those methods would be thrown out of court," John told her.

Kate made a totally unfeminine gesture with the middle finger of her left hand.

Barry smiled at her and winked. "Well, boys, like Ted Fabrello told me, the opera ain't over until the fat lady sings.''

"Damn right," Kate said.

John and Jackson and Ralph moved toward the front door at Barry's wave. Barry told them, "We've got a load to deliver. You boys play it your way, I'll play it mine. See you.''

He closed the door.

Barry looked at Kate. "We'll stay on 95 down to South Carolina and then cut west into Georgia. That OK with you?''

She shrugged. "Suits me.''

"We'll lay over in South Carolina for twenty-four hours.''

Again she shrugged. "We've got the time. But it'll be crowding it. Why the layover?''

"'Cause there is a twenty-four-hour wait in South Carolina.''

"A twenty-four-hour wait for what, Barry?''

"After we file for a marriage license.''

It was an easy run down to Columbia. There, Kate and Barry filed for a license, saw the sights while they waited, then got married.

Rolling out before dawn, on Interstate 20, Kate said, "First time, I had me a big church wedding. You?''

"Absolutely. My family was all smiles. Her folks sat there looking like they'd just swallowed a peck of pickles."

"What do you reckon your kids will think of me?"

"They'll love you, I hope. If they don't? . . . One mistake parents make, I think, is trying to live their lives for their kids. I think parents should give their kids love, direction, values, and discipline. I haven't had much of a hand in raising my kids. But they're pretty good kids. I think they'll like you."

I hope, he silently added.

About fifty miles inside Georgia, Barry and Kate cut southwest on a state road. They changed highways twice, finally reaching their destination off a county road.

Instant replay.

The closed compound, the armed guards, the low block buildings, the secrecy . . . and the silent horror of it all.

"Memorize the inside of the compound, Kate," Barry said. "When we get back in the truck, write down as much of it as you can remember."

"Just like you did up in Maine?"

"Yes."

"Why?"

"Because we're going to come back. Legally, or illegally."

"I kinda hoped you'd say that. But the way this country's laws are now, I bet it's gonna be illegally."

"That's just dandy with me," Barry replied, a hard grimness to this voice.

They pulled out just after lunch, deadheading back to New Orleans. At the cafe in Georgia, Barry had called the terminal; all the drivers were there, sitting around, drinking coffee, playing cards, killing time. Drawing government money for doing nothing. And none of them liked it.

Jim Carson told Barry that Fabrello had sent one of his men around with a message: Fabrello was going on an extended vacation abroad.

"He give a reason?" Barry asked.

"You read a paper or watched any news the last couple of days?" Carson asked.

No.

Jim had told him that the press had gotten wind of a big Mafia meet in New York City. Fabrello had been ordered to clean up his house—any way he saw fit. Fabrello had not been mentioned in the newspaper story, but all concerned knew who the paper was talking about.

Fabrello had cleaned house, all right—starting with Bobby Bulgari and his operation. Bulgari had been found dead in his Biloxi apartment, an apparent suicide. Sure it was. Four of Bulgari's lieutenants had been killed in a shootout with some unknown parties on a lonely Mississippi back road. Another shootout had taken place in an after-hours nightspot in south Mississippi. No survivors.

Bulgari's little empire had crumbled.

Barry told Kate about it as they drove.

"What does this mean to us? Now?" she asked.

"I think it just might throw everything into mild panic. Now my partner is going to have to look for someone else to lay the blame on."

He was conscious of Kate's eyes searching his face. "And who do you think he might pick?" she asked.

"Yeah, Kate. That thought just entered my mind."

"He'd have access to all your company books, wouldn't he?"

"Yeah," Barry replied glumly.

"I kind of like being Mrs. Rivers," Kate said. "I'd rather not be a widow this quick."

"I'll do my best to try to stay alive, ma'am."

20

"Seems like to me," Bullwhip said, "if you were under suspicion, our SST contract would have been pulled. Don't it to you, Mr. Rivers?"

"Not if they were tryin' to set him up," Lady Lou offered. "And if your fat little partner is the kingpin of all this mess, he'd have contacts within the agency who hands out the SST contracts, right?"

"It would appear that way. It's going to be Big Casino time shortly, people. And I'm not going to risk your lives in this thing. So I'm canceling the contract."

"Can't," Jim said shortly.

"What do you mean, Jim?"

"We're under contract to make a certain number of runs. We haven't even dented the schedule yet. I went back and reread the contract. They've got us in a hard bind, Barry."

Barry shook his head. "Not we, Jim. *Me*. You can all quit

this morning and I'll rehire you under a new contract tomorrow. How about that?''

"Some of 'em might go for that," Swamp Wolf said. "But not me. I'm in this 'til the end."

"Me, too," Beer Butt said. "Call it personal reasons. I'm stayin'."

"I lost a boy in Vietnam," Lady Lou said. "I'd hate to think he died so something this slimy could continue. I'm in."

"I fought in Korea," Beaver Buster said. "I'm stayin' with this."

"I know you fought gonorrhea," Grits said. "I didn't know about Korea."

"Watch your mouth!" Lou warned him over the laughter. "You in or out, Grits?"

"Do you have to ask?" Grits said, a mournful expression on his face. "Plumb insultin'."

"Well, I guess I'd better tag along and look after you," his partner, Cornbread, said. "You're so absentminded you're liable to forget where you parked your truck without me to show you."

"I don't like what's happening to those veterans," Cajun said. "You'd have to shoot me to get me to quit now, Mr. Rivers."

"I've gotten used to your ugly face, Panty Snatcher," Cottonmouth said to his partner. "I'd get lonesome without you."

"You try to kiss me, I'll knock the crap outta you!" Panty Snatcher warned him. "Bad enough I have to listen to you try to sing. Yeah . . . count me in, Mr. Rivers."

Coyote said, "My momma was born in Mexico. I still got lots of family down there. I ain't never seen none of them, but that don't make no difference. Anybody that would do what these doctors are doin' to another human bein' don't deserve to live. I'm stayin'."

"I didn't know you was half Mexican," Bullwhip said, lying through his false teeth. "I thought you was an A-rab."

Barry let them insult each other. He had suspected before any of this had begun that they would all stay.

When they had wound down, Snake said, "That's a right-nice-lookin' ring on your hand, Kate. Jim tells me you and Mr. Rivers got hitched. Now, I don't want you to take this the wrong way, but maybe you'd better sit this one out."

Kate told him where to go, how to get there, and what to stick up a certain part of his anatomy while traveling the route.

"I kinda figured you'd take it the wrong way," Snake responded.

"Kate . . ." Barry said.

"Don't start," she warned him. "I go where you go. Hell, somebody's got to teach you how to drive a truck."

"We'll talk about it later," Barry said.

"You'll be talkin' to an empty side of the bed, too. The talkin' is over. Let's look at the travelin' orders and get this show on the road." She glared at Barry. "You got any objections?"

He didn't have a one.

Barry felt in his guts it was a setup. He read the orders, received by registered mail, three times. Still, the feeling would not leave him.

His father was up and about and sitting in his office when Barry handed him the traveling orders. Big Joe read them, shrugged, and placed the orders back on his son's desk. "They look pretty simple to me, boy."

"Yeah, don't they. We'll all be hauling super-secret fighter-plane electronic gear. Pick up the load in Tacoma and truck it to Texas. Easy run. But I don't like it."

"You'd rather be shooting up those, well, medical facilities, wouldn't you, boy?"

"I damn sure would!"

"You're not the law. Right now, you're a truck driver. Let the authorities handle those other places. You're not exactly battin' a thousand with your hunches, you know?"

"I'm not striking out each time at bat, either," Barry reminded his dad.

"No. I'll say you did a few things right. You got yourself a good wife."

The tension vanished between father and son. Barry smiled and said, "Think you could convince her to stay out of this thing?"

"I'd sooner French-kiss a bull 'gator than try to do that, boy. Kate's mind is made up and she's goin' with you. Period. Best thing you can do is realize that and get off the dime."

Barry nodded his agreement. "I've got some decisions to make, Pop. Heavy ones."

"Kate?"

"No. Jack, my partner."

"The law will take care of him."

"Maybe. But I rather doubt he'll ever see the inside of a jail cell. Jack is up to his ass in this stinking operation, but I can't shake the feeling that he is not alone at the top."

"You're not still thinking this Linda O'Day has something to do with it?"

Barry waved that aside. "No. I was wrong about her. I admit it. Somebody set me up—or is attempting to—and Jack is part of it. But, Dad, Jack is a city boy. Now, he can design a weapons system that is unequalled. He designs them, I sell them. But he doesn't know a bob truck from a wheelbarrow. You see what I'm getting at?"

"Maybe," the elder Rivers said. "And it's on that little bit of suspicion you're basing your theory that someone else is beside him at the top?"

"That and a gut feeling."

"Boy, you're gettin' paranoid."

"Actually, considering all that's happened, I'm happier than I've been in years."

"I can understand part of that statement."

"Certainly Kate is playing a large part in it. But it's more than that."

"How much money are you worth, boy?" the father asked. "Not that it's any of my business," he quickly added.

"On paper I'm worth several million dollars. If I had to do it, I could probably put my hands on, oh, half a million bucks very quickly."

"A nice chunk of money. I'm worth about the same, give or take a few hundred thousand. Before you married Kate, who stood to inherit your money?"

"My kids, you, Donna."

Surprise sprang into Big Joe's eyes. "Aren't you leaving out somebody?"

"Who?"

"Well, boy, your *brother*. Paul, that's who."

"Screw Paul. He doesn't like me any more than I like him. I have no use for Paul, Dad. None whatsoever."

"When's the last time you two got together?"

"Five years ago. Right here in New Orleans. You remember it. What are you getting at?"

The man shrugged. "Nothing. I'd just like to see the two of you bury the hatchet, that's all. It's not right for brothers to dislike each other; at least not the way you two feel."

"We'll never be close, Dad. Paul dislikes my lifestyle and I personally think he's flirting with communism—or something very close to it."

"He does have some ... strange views," the father agreed. "But damned if I can figure out where he come up on them. *Quel dommage.*"

"Pitiful is more like it," Barry said. "How's your private little army, Dad?" He grinned.

Big Joe grimaced. "Can't move without fallin' over them. Must be costin' Fabrello a fortune."

"I'm glad you've got them, regardless of the cost."

Big Joe grinned. "Tell you the truth, boy, so am I."

After his father had left the office, driven home by one of his appointed bodyguards, Barry leaned back in his chair and studied the ceiling for a moment, deep in thought.

What had his dad been getting at, inquiring about his wealth, who was in his will? And what about his brother, Paul?

He left the office and drove to a pay phone, placing a call to the detective agency he'd used before. He talked to the owner of the agency, asking him to very quietly find out anything and everything about one Paul Rivers, attorney, in Baton Rouge.

He'd call back in about a week. Don't mail anything. Verbal reports only. OK?

Fine.

Jesus, Barry thought. Maybe Dad is right. Maybe I am getting paranoid. Paul wouldn't have the guts to be involved in anything like this mess.

Crap! He was spending his money for nothing, having Paul investigated.

But . . . at least he could clear the air concerning Paul. That alone would be worth the money.

He wanted to call back to D.C.—see what was happening. But he felt he knew. Nothing would be shaking. The law was so goddamned ponderous. But he guessed it had to be, to protect the innocent.

He drove the outskirts of the city aimlessly, in his pickup. Something was nagging at him, digging at his guts with dull claws, attempting to gain a firmer hold. But Barry could not pull it closer, could not bring it into full mental light. What the hell was it?

Something he had heard?

Something he remembered?

Something he merely suspected?

He didn't know. But it was there. Had been there for several days. Whatever it was, it was slowly gaining strength. But not fast enough.

He fought the elusive feelings away and concentrated on the run due to begin at dawn tomorrow. The upcoming long haul was going to be very dangerous. They would all have to be very careful. Alert every mile, coming and going. It was going to be a waiting game. Like stepping into a dark room, knowing a rattlesnake was in there. But you just didn't know where.

All you could do was wait for the rattle.

21

To Barry, the scene was reminiscent of those few moments before combat troops mounted up for a night jump into unknown territory behind enemy lines. Wives or girl friends—in Lou's case, a boyfriend—had driven the drivers to the terminal before dawn. The tractors were rumbling, warming up, while the drivers stood on the loading docks, smoking, sipping coffee, and talking quietly.

There would be no outriders or drag vehicles on this long run. Nine rigs rolling in a loose convoy. All radio-equipped, with CB and shortwave radios. Barry had given dispatch their route and was just about to tell the drivers to mount up when the headlights of a car cut the semidarkness, pocked only by running lights of the nine trucks.

Barry recognized one of Fabrello's men. He walked to the docks and motioned Barry to one side.

Barry squatted down on the concrete lip as the man began speaking in low tones.

"We got a message from Mr. Fabrello last night. Part of it concerns you. Part of what you and him talked about is fact now. Some government people is up to their asses in this thing. Your partner is gettin' ready to set you up for a hard fall. But your partner has a partner too. Besides you. Contracts has been put out on Big Joe, Kate, your sister, and your kids . . ."

Barry felt a shiver move up and down his spine as his stomach suddenly turned queasy.

". . . Mr. Fabrello says we'll do our best to cover them all like a blanket. But we're spread kinda thin. New York don't wanna get involved in this matter. They say they're gettin' strong smells that it would be to their best interest to back off. Mr. Fabrello's got the man in Houston by the balls, so your sister is gonna be OK. Your kids up east . . ." He shrugged. "I don't know. If you know some private guns, you'd better call them and put your kids under twenty-four-hour protection. Mr. Fabrello says this whole thing is gonna be resolved sometime in the next week or ten days. And he says for you to watch your ass, in all directions."

"I'll get on the horn right now and arrange private security for Missy and Barry. If I can convince my ex-wife of it."

"You'd better," the man said ominously. "All bets are down and the pot's right."

"Big Joe will be OK?"

"Right. No sweat there."

"Kate will be with me. I guess she's as safe there as anywhere?"

The man shrugged noncommittally.

"And Donna will be protected?"

"Like a baby."

The other drivers were watching quietly, staying a respectable distance away.

"Aren't you leaving someone out?" Barry asked Fabrello's man.

The man's eyes were bleak. He said nothing.

"Like my brother?"

"Your brother is a shit! And if you didn't think so, you wouldn't be having your favorite detective agency run him."

"Now, how in the hell do you know about that?"

The man smiled for the first time. "Hell, Rivers. It's mob-owned."

Barry sat down on the lip of the dock. "Maybe we'd better compare notes, Mister . . . ?"

"Al will do fine. What compare notes? You wanna know why the boss is doin' this? Hell, he likes you, Rivers. And he likes Big Joe."

"That's not exactly what I meant," Barry said dryly.

"Your shitty little brother got himself in a hard bind three, four years ago. He needed money. He started playing footsie with Bobby Bulgari. Your fat partner, Jack, has been supplying guns to the eastern mob for years. His old lady is a coke freak. Free guns, free nose candy. Then Bulgari come up with a plan to infiltrate the SST business. There was a big sit-down in New York about it. The central committee nixed the plan. We don't wanna fuck too much with the government. Mr. Fabrello explained that to you. All the capos thought it was settled. But Bobby went ahead on his own. Very quietly. With your partner's help. Then this Linda O'Day broad done some snoopin' and found some bad smells. But she only scratched the surface. She was about to get burned when you come into the picture. And you didn't come into it by accident. Don't never believe that, Rivers. Fat-assed Jack needed a pigeon and looked at you. Jack knew some hungry government people. They knew about this medical thing with vets and wetbacks. Jack and the agents got together with your little brother. It was a good way to bring in dope, on the SSTs. Then your little brother got really greedy. You're worth a lot of money, and so is Big Joe. If he was the sole survivor, he gets it all. That's it in a nutshell."

"Who is funding this research on the vets?"

Al shrugged. "The government, I guess. That ain't none of our concern. Mr. Fabrello thinks it stinks, he won the Silver Star in Korea with the Marines, but there is no mob connection with this medical crap."

"Thanks, Al."

"Watch your ass, man. Oh, you need anything?"

"Like what?"

"Bazookas, flame throwers, mortars, machine guns . . . stuff like that?"

Despite it all, Barry had to laugh. Al grinned along with the laughter. Barry said, "You know, you people could take over the world if you really tried."

"Oh, we don't want the whole world. Just a reasonably profitable piece of it."

Al turned and walked away.

Barry had laid it all out for his drivers, all the while wondering if one of them might be in Fabrello's pocket. He didn't think so, but with the mob, one never knew.

"Last chance, people," Barry said. "If any of you want out, take off. No one will blame you for it."

The drivers stood and stared at him. No one moved. No one spoke. Barry felt that no one would pull out at this late stage, but it was a question he had to ask.

"All right, gang," Barry said. "Let's do it."

* * *

They rolled and rumbled out in predawn darkness, heading for Houston.

"I don't think I ever want to meet your little brother," Kate said, behind the wheel. "I might be tempted to put a boot up his butt."

"If all that Al told me proves out, I'm going to meet him one more time," Barry told her, a deadly grimness in his tone.

Kate knew what that grimness meant; she did not pursue it, only saying, "I hope it never comes to that, Barry."

Barry was silent for a few miles. He had called his ex-wife, telling her to expect protection for the kids. He could not tell her the real reason, so he lied, making up some kidnapping threat he had received against the kids.

She was as haughty as ever, disdainfully turning down his offer. She said she would arrange protection of her own.

"Julie," Barry had said, "listen to me. Please. I know the type of people you'll get. They won't stand a chance going up against these hardcases."

"Oh? So you know who they are, then?"

"I know their types, Julie. You don't. You've no realistic concept of the real world. And I don't mean that in any insulting way. It's just that you've been insulated all your life. Please let me arrange some guns for you."

"*Guns,* Barry? I think not. Mother and Father will see to the children's safety. Quite adequately, I might add."

He was losing, and he knew it. They had never been able to communicate. Time had not improved that. "Julie, think of the kids. Put aside your dislike of me, and think of them."

She had then hung up on him.

"God, Barry," Kate said. "What kind of a person is she?"

"A very good mother, really. She just hates me."

"What'd you do, beat her?" She grinned.

"The thought occurred to me, and you can believe that."

"What will you do now? About the kids, I mean?"

"Say a silent prayer. I'm in a bind with this thing. I can't go to the police; I have no proof that anything is about to happen. I can't tell them I heard it from the Mafia, for Christ's sake." They both laughed at that. "Julie's father is a snob, but he's a hard-nosed snob. He'll take one look at those playboys she'll gather around her and kick them out of the house. I hope. Then—again, I'm hoping—he'll call some real men in. Men who won't hesitate to shoot first and ask questions later."

"And if he doesn't?"

"I'm trying not to think about that."

Barry took over at Houston, heading north-northwest on Interstate 45. They rolled in a loose convoy, switching CB channels often, never talking on the truckers' channel, 19.

They spent the night just outside of Dallas, abiding by their five-hundred-mile-per-day limit. Barry was going to stay with the preplanned route all the way, never straying from it.

He did not know how the trouble coming at them would arrive—just that it would come. And, surprisingly, he was not shocked at learning his brother was involved in the slime. He said as much to Kate.

"Why, Barry?" she asked.

"For all his grandiose, so-called ideals, Paul was always a sneak. But I'll say this much for him: nothing ever came easy for Paul. He always resented me. I thought he'd out-grow it; obviously, he didn't. Paul had to struggle through school. I never cracked a book in high school. Paul took after his mother in build. I took after Dad. He wasn't big enough to play sports; they just came naturally to me. Not that I gave a shit for sports, because I didn't.''

"Then why did you play?"

Barry grinned. "Girls. Many teenage girls can't see past the end of their noses. Which is probably not their fault, when one takes into consideration all the bullshit hype about jocks.''

"I never gave a damn for jocks," Kate said. "I always admired the boys who had some sense. Not that any of them ever looked at me," she added, a wistful note in her voice.''

"I can't believe that!" Barry said.

"I came from the wrong side of town, Barry. Drunk for a dad; never could hold a job. My mother barely made a livin' slingin' hash. The wrong type of boys looked at me for all the wrong reasons.''

Kate had never talked much about her life. Barry waited.

"It wasn't easy," she finally said. "I quit school in the tenth grade. Got a job; got a series of jobs. None of them payin' more than minimum wage. Knocked around. Finally got married. He used to beat the shit out of me. I guess you know what happened.''

"I know."

"So we don't have to talk no more about it, right?"

"Right."

"I love you, Barry Rivers," she said. "But I got a funny feelin', too.''

"That's what love is, Kate." Barry smiled at her. "A funny feeling.''

"Yeah, I know. But this is something else."

"You want to tell me about it?"

"Not much to tell. I just got a bad feelin', that's all."

And she would say no more about it.

The convoy rolled into Salina, Kansas, and the drivers checked into a motel. The motel manager wasn't too thrilled about all the rigs in his parking lot, but his only visible objection was a few very dark glances. Every time he would turn his back, Kate would shoot him the bird.

On the way to their rooms, Cottonmouth hesitated, then stopped.

"Something wrong?" Panty Snatcher asked.

"My boots is hurtin' my feet. I'm gonna get my other pair outta the sleeper. Be back in a minute."

Barry opened the door at the knock. Cottonmouth stood there, his spare boots in his hand. His face was tight with anger.

"What's wrong?" Barry asked.

"I noticed the liner pulled out behind my boots, Barry. In the storage area up top. This is what I found." He held out a clear plastic bag. The bag contained white powder. Barry knew what it was.

Cocaine.

"Warn the others," Barry said. "Have them check their sleepers very carefully. Check boots, clothing, blankets, luggage, everything. If they find anything that looks like this, flush it down the toilet, then flush the bags. Don't spill a particle of it on the floor. I've got a hunch we're going to have cops all over us in a very short time. Move it, Cottonmouth. Kate, check our rig. Quickly but carefully. I'll take care of this junk."

The drivers all reported finding bags of dope in their rigs. They flushed the dope down the commode, then flushed the bags behind that. They then showered and dressed for dinner.

Eighteen very pissed-off truckers.

22

The dining room of the motel was not very busy when the drivers arrived, took their tables, and ordered dinner.

"Supper," Kate said.

"Dinner," Barry corrected.

"Grub," Saltmeat settled it.

"Plainclothes cops comin' in," Grits said, cutting his eyes toward the archway to the dining room.

The cops took tables about the dining area, effectively sealing the room off. A man walked up to Barry's table and sat down. Uninvited.

Kate looked at him. "Something on your mind, buddy?" Kate said.

"Watch your mouth," the cop warned.

"Screw you!" she popped back.

"Take it easy," Barry said, putting a stop to it. He locked eyes with the cop. He fished in his pocket and handed the man his orange card. "We're SST drivers, Mr. Policeman, and by that bulge on the right side of your jacket, I can only assume that's a gun. If you're not a cop, then you're a hood. Which is it?''

"Lieutenant Mattlock. State police. You're Barry Rivers?''

"I am.''

"I have a search warrant signed by a judge, Mr. Rivers. The warrant empowers me to conduct a search of all your trucks.''

"Your state warrant doesn't mean a thing to me, Mattlock. Show me a federal warrant.''

Mattlock smiled and handed Barry a warrant signed by a federal district judge. "That gentleman sitting right over there''—he cut his eyes—"is a federal marshal. Do I have to say more?''

"You gonna read us our rights, Mr. Po-liceman?'' Coyote asked.

"Not yet. Maybe never. It all depends on what I find.''

"Dirty socks, dirty drawers,'' Beer Butt told him. "And if you got sinus problems, just take a whiff of my partner's socks. You'll never be troubled again.''

The cop's smile was thin.

"Do you object if we eat while you're prowling through our possessions? Or should we go outside with you to see that you don't plant anything in our rigs?''

"Do whatever you damn well please to do,'' Mattlock told him.

"I think I'll just go with you,'' Barry said.

It was full dark when the police finished their search of the rigs. They had found no contraband of any kind.

"Now show me the other warrant,'' Barry said.

The cop was angry, but managed to conceal it quite well. "This warrant?" he said, handing Barry a paper.

Barry looked at it. A warrant to search their rooms. "That's the one. Help yourself, Mattlock."

"I fully intend to do just that."

The cops, naturally, turned up nothing in any of the drivers' rooms. But it was not because they didn't try.

With the motel residents and manager settled back down after the minor disruptions, and most of the police gone, Barry and Kate stood outside with the state police and federal marshal.

"Are you satisfied now?" Barry asked Mattlock.

"Yes, we are, Mr. Rivers."

Barry had been promoted to *Mister* status. "Now there are just two more things you have to do."

"Oh?"

"Apologize, and *leave.*"

Mattlock gave him a sharp glance. "I suppose I can understand your irritation."

"You suppose? My, my, but you are a well of understanding, aren't you? Who accused us of carrying dope, Lieutenant?"

"I haven't any idea, Mr. Rivers. I only carried out the warrants."

"Sure you did," Barry said sarcastically. "And I don't suppose there'd be much point in my contacting an attorney to try to force that information out of anybody?"

"You certainly have my permission to try," the cop said blandly.

Barry laughed at him.

"Good night, Mr. Rivers," Mattlock said. "And thank you for your understanding."

* * *

Barry awakened before Kate, an idea forming in his mind. He was not going to wait for the slow-motion efforts of the criminal justice system. He slipped gently from the bed and stepped out into the predawn darkness of Kansas.

He was surprised to see several of his drivers standing outside their rooms. He walked to them. "Can't sleep?" he asked.

Saltmeat's smile was grim. "Me and the boys been talkin'. Goin' back over some things we picked up here and there over the past months."

"Such as?"

"Where them renegade drivers maybe been pickin' up the Mexicans."

"Oh?"

"Yeah. If nothin' else good comes out of this mess, we'd like to bust up that operation."

"I'm listening."

"Guy I'm thinkin' of calls himself Cowboy. Lives just outside of San Antonio. And lives damn well for a trucker. He don't make that many runs. But the ones he does make is always up to northern California. He's got a buddy who lives pretty damn well, too. Calls himself Bad Ass. Bad Ass don't run nowwhere except up to Minnesota. And there's another one calls himself Slick. He runs up to northern Maine. You beginnin' to get the picture?"

"Yeah. They're independents?"

"Right. And I been thinkin', the way the economy is now, there ain't no way they could live as good as they do makin' no more runs than they do."

Barry looked first at Saltmeat, then at the others gathered around him. "I'm not going to wait for our system of justice to step in, boys. Bearing that in mind, you want to hear the rest?''

No one moved. No one spoke. Just stood and looked at Barry.

''If you throw in with me in this crazy, not-yet-worked-out plan of mine, you could all lose your license; maybe never drive a truck again. Good chance of going to prison.''

''You sure do talk a lot without sayin' nothin','' Cornbread said.

''Yeah,'' Coyote said. ''Let's stop all the sparrin' and get to the main event.''

''Well, you hairy-legs better goddamn sure include us in all this jawin'!'' Lady Lou spoke from behind the gathered drivers.

All looked up and around. Kate stood with Lou, both of them wearing irritated looks.

''Now look, ladies,'' Barry began. ''You—''

''I'm a truck driver, Mr. Rivers,'' Lou said. ''I run the same risks any other driver does, day in and day out. I signed on with Rivers Trucking, and I'll pull my weight. If you don't like it, fire me.''

''I'm your wife, Barry Rivers,'' Kate said. ''I go where you go. That's it.''

Barry smiled at the women. He slowly nodded his head. ''OK, people. Here is it.''

23

The convey rolled out of Kansas and into Colorado on Interstate 70. At Denver they connected with Interstate 25 and began climbing north, rolling at a steady 55 mph. About halfway between Denver and Cheyenne, they pulled over for the night, one person sleeping in each rig, the other partner in a motel room.

They wanted no more repeats of the events in Kansas.

They were rolling again before dawn, cutting west at Cheyenne on Interstate 80. It was an easy run to Salt Lake City, and they decided to stop there. If they had been followed, or if someone, some team, was keeping them under surveillance, none of the truckers had been able to spot them.

And that made them all a bit uneasy.

Just as Barry and Kate were getting ready to go to bed, a knock came on the door. A soft knock.

Beer Butt motioned Barry outside. "Ol' boy calls himself

Utah Slim is checkin' in up front, Barry. He usually runs with Slick.''

"What's he driving?"

"That Peterbilt over yonder. The one with all the chrome on it.'' He pointed. "Goddamn candy wagon. Look at all them lights.''

"You check it out?''

"Swamp Wolf is over there now. Here he comes.''

"I think he's runnin' light,'' Swamp Wolf said. "I don't like Slim and I don't trust him. He's a sneaky bastard. Do anything for money. He's been in and out of trouble all his miserable life.''

Mustang joined the group. He rolled his chew of Red Man around in his mouth and said, "I whipped Slim's ass over in Missouri one night. 'Bout a year or so back. It's all comin' to me, now.''

"What do you mean?'' Barry asked.

"He was braggin' about doin' a service for his country. Something about findin' a use for certain people. He didn't say much more about that. And that wasn't what we fought about. We fought over a woman. But I think what he said ties in.''

"Go get him,'' Barry told Cajun. "You need any help with him?''

"Shhitt!'' Cajun said contemptuously.

Barry grinned. "He's all yours. I'll meet you back at my room.''

The truckers' rooms were all together, on the ground floor, starting at one end of the complex. They were secure left and right. But Barry worried about the rooms being occupied above them.

"Go check it out,'' he told Cornbread.

Cornbread was back in a few moments. "All empty.

Looks like the room right above this one is being repainted. The next two are empty."

Cajun shoved a very wide-eyed-looking man into the room. Kate and Lou were in the dining room. At their own suggestion.

"What the hell's goin' on here, man?" Utah Slim asked Barry. He was doing his best tough-man act, but it was falling flat, and falling on tougher ears than his.

Utah Slim was scared.

"Let's talk awhile, Slim," Barry said. "Have a seat." He pointed to a chair.

"I ain't got nothing to say to you, mister," Slim blustered.

"Well, then, how about this suggestion, Slim." Barry smiled at him. "Why don't I call the FBI office in Salt Lake City and invite them out here?"

"Uh . . . why would you wanna do that?" Slim asked, his face flushing.

"Because our two agencies try to work together. You see, there was a breakout up in northern Maine. A couple of people got free. They talked. Guess who they talked about?"

"Uh . . . I don't know nothin' about Maine. And what agencies are you talkin' about?"

"I'm with Treasury, Slim." Barry had leveled with his people, telling them of his Treasury connection.

"Lemme see some ID," Slim said, his voice suddenly very shaky.

Barry produced his card. Slim's fingers were trembling as he held the ID card. "You got a warrant for me?"

"No. Not yet." Barry continued the bluff. "I wanted to hold up on that."

Slim's eyes took on a fox's glint. "What d'you mean?"

"I think you know."

"You can guarantee me no jail time?"

"No guarantees." Barry had watched as many cop movies as anyone. "But I can put in a good word for you."

Slim looked around the crowded room. "All these guys workin' for Treasury?"

"In a manner of speaking. They brought you here, didn't they?"

Slim nodded his head. His shoulders slumped. "I knowed we was gonna get caught sooner or later. I told Cowboy it was time to quit. He wouldn't listen. Can I sit down? My knees is a little weak."

Not a trucker present wanted any supper after hearing Utah Slim's story. Cottonmouth summed up everybody's feelings by going into the bathroom and throwing up.

"Jesus Christ!" Cottonmouth said. "I ain't never heard nothing that rotten."

"Sorry son of a bitch!" Coyote said, glaring at Slim.

The experiments, according to Slim, were not confined solely to mentally ill Vietnam vets. They included Mexican aliens, men and women from Central America, runaways picked up on the streets and highways, homeless men and women. Kids. Dogs.

Sick.

"Stay with him," Barry said. He went looking for Kate. She paled when he told her what he planned to do.

"That's the way it's going down, Kate. Beer Butt will look after you. It's got to be this way. I think you understand."

"I understand, but I don't have to like it."

"I'll see you in Texas, baby."

* * *

"You're fuckin' *crazy!*" Utah Slim said, after Barry had told him what they were going to do.

"You drive, Slim," Barry told him. "And if you try to pull anything, I'll gut-shoot you and leave you on the side of the road to die. You understand all that?"

"Crazy bastard!"Slim said. "I think you'd do it, too."

"Believe it," Barry assured him, his voice steel hard and very menacing.

"Where's that confession I wrote out, Mr. Rivers?"

"In the mailbox, heading back to Washington, along with details of where we're going and what we're going to do. All the names, the dates you remembered, the places you rolled to and from, the locations of the medical facilities, and your partners. If you turn sour on me, that confession goes to the feds. Understood?"

"I'm with you, Mr. Rivers," Utah Slim assured him. "Think about it. I'm lookin' at kidnapping, murder, torture, dope running, and probably a dozen other charges. And you got me in a box with the lid screwed down tight. Put yourself in my place; what would you do?"

"Looking at the electric chair, Slim, as you are, I'd give it one hundred and ten percent."

"You got it, Mr. Rivers. If we can pull all this craziness off, what happens to me?"

"You walk out free. No charges. I tear up the confession."

Utah Slim geared the Peterbilt. "Let's do it, Mr. Rivers."

"South. To Texas."

They had rolled out just before midnight, looking at eleven hundred miles down to south Texas. None of the drivers had liked the plan; none of the drivers trusted Utah Slim. But Barry was the boss.

They stood, a quiet group, watching the Peterbilt rumble out into the night.

"I'm gonna get on the horn," Cornbread said. "I seen Woodchuck's rig just before we pulled in. Heard some ol' boys talkin'. They said he was headin' down Texas way. Him and Big Foot and Hawkeye."

"And . . . ?" Lady Lou asked.

"We always talk about takin' care of our own . . . 'bout time we lived up to that mouth."

"I know some ol' boys live not far from Fort Stockton," Panty Snatcher said. "I'll give them a call."

"Good," Lou said. "Tell 'em all they have to do is look for a goddamned Christmas tree rollin' through the night."

Soft yet tough laughter in the night. Lady Lou seldom cussed. A sure sign she was mad as hell.

"What ol' boys you know down there?" Snake asked.

"Dolittle, Shiny Hiney, Montana."

"Pretty tough ol' boys, all right," Grits agreed. "And since they all about to lose their trucks to the banks, they won't mind tearin' 'em up helpin' someone."

Panty Snatcher grinned. "That's what I mean."

"Let's get some sleep," Jim ordered. "We still got to get to Tacoma."

"Yeah," Kate said, her eyes searching the void of night for her man. "And then to Texas."

Utah Slim was, so far, true to his word. Barry even slept for a few hours. When he awakened, they were on the right road, holding true, heading for Texas. And for the first showdown with what Barry had called the ultimate evil.

"Want me to take it?" Barry asked.

"I'll take her on down to Shiprock, hand it over to you there. I'll sleep 'til Albuquerque, then relieve you."

Barry poured them coffee from a Stanley thermos, handing Slim a cup.

They sipped and rode in silence for a few miles. It seemed to Barry that Slim wanted to talk but didn't know quite how to start. "Something on your mind, Slim?"

"Yeah. But right off the bat I'll say I ain't gonna offer up any excuses for what we done."

"No one asked for any."

"You really mean it when you said I could walk free when this is over?"

"Yes. I gave my word. But we're going to destroy all those so-called medical centers. And there is a good chance none of us will walk away from any of it."

"I heard that. Don't make no difference to me. Not now, no ways. Tell you the truth, I feel like I just took a shower and come out clean. That make any sense to you?"

"Yes."

"I backed into it. Pure blind greed. Easy money. And that ain't excuses. Just the truth." He reached for his wallet and fumbled out a piece of paper, handing it to Barry. "Read it, Mr. Rivers."

"How about making it Barry, Slim?"

"Suits me. You'll see that thing ain't signed. But you can see the direction I was tryin' to head."

Barry read the poorly typed paper. It was what Slim had told them, back at the motel. The paper was not heavily creased, so he had not been carrying it long.

"If your . . . friends, for want of a better word, had found you with this, they'd have killed you, Slim."

"Don't I know it."

"Why did you write this?"

" 'Cause I was gettin' disgusted with myself. I wanted out, but I didn't know how to do it."

The man's voice was choked and emotion-charged. Barry believed him. It would take a slimy sort to take in the business of human grief for very long and not feel dirty. "I believe you, Slim."

"There ain't one livin' soul to give a shit whether or not I live or die. But before I do die, I wanna do something."

"Something right, for a change?" Barry asked.

"I think it's right." Utah Slim reached down between the seats.

Barry tensed.

When Slim's hand reappeared, he had his fingers wrapped around the butt of a .38. With a smile, he pointed the muzzle at Barry.

24

"Careless of me, wasn't it, Slim?" Barry asked, feeling he was only seconds away from getting a hot slug tearing through his guts.

"Yeah, it was." Slim reversed the weapon and handed it, butt-first, to Barry. "No offense meant, Barry, but I been tryin' to get Kate's jeans off for years. Me and a lot of other ol' boys. If she picked you, then you're one hell of a good man. I'm honored to roll with you."

Barry smiled. "Put the gun in your pocket, Slim. I got a hunch you're going to need it before this is over."

Slim nodded. "Finally got me a straight-shootin' partner. I'll stick, Barry. Don't never doubt it."

"What happens now?" Barry asked. "Do you kiss me?"

Slim looked startled; then a slow grin spread over his rugged face.

Both men spent the next couple of miles laughing.

* * *

As they drove, stopping only when they absolutely had to do it—food, fuel, scales—Barry and Slim firmed up their plans.

Slim was returning from a legit run up to Billings. He was to take his time and eventually wind his way down to Van Horn, Texas. He was to receive instructions there, general delivery at the post office.

"Any idea where you might go?" Barry asked.

"Oh, yeah. Just north of the Big Bend. Not far from 385. Soon as I pick up the load of Mexicans, I'll cut north on 285 and head for Colorado. There's one of them centers there."

"When we get through destroying your past employer's little playhouse in south Texas, we'll deal with the center in Colorado."

"That suits me just fine, Barry. But I gotta warn you, we're gonna be two against about twenty."

"Hell, Slim, we got them outnumbered!"

The truck drivers gathered at a rest area on Interstate 10, in Texas. They took their thermos bottles of coffee and sacks of sandwiches to a table away from tourists out of four-wheelers and sipped and ate and quietly talked.

"It's a damned disgrace," Horsefly said. "I still can't believe all that Panty Snatcher told me."

"I can believe it," Dolittle said. "It all fits with the bits and pieces of rumors we've all heard over the past couple of years."

"That we been ignorin'." Montana spoke the words bitterly.

"We had no way of knowin' that any of it was true,"

Horsefly replied. "Now that we know that it is, we can by God do something about it."

"Panty Snatcher spoke real highly of this Barry Rivers. Must be a hell of a man for that old grump to think that much of him."

"Married Kate, didn't he?" Dolittle said with a grin, knowing he was rubbing a tender spot.

"I don't even wanna think about that," Montana said glumly.

"And Lady Lou said he was one hell of a nice guy." Shiny Hiney spoke around a mouthful of sandwich. "And she don't speak too highly of too many men."

"I've done some shitty things in my life," Horsefly spoke. "But anybody that would do what Panty Snatcher told us about is a lowlife son of a bitch."

"All right, all right!" Montana said impatiently. "Let's quit waltzin' around and get to it. Rivers and Utah Slim will be in this area in about eight hours. We got to get organized and plan this thing out." He spread a map on the table. He put a blunt finger on a spot. "Right there is where we'll meet 'em. I'd rather wreck my rig than give it back to the bank. Hell, I might even give the damn thing to them wetbacks and let them take it back to Mexico. I'll say it was stole."

"I was gonna do that!" Horsefly said.

"Well, we'll both do it. Who cares? You guys go on back and kiss your wives and girlfriends good-bye and get your guns. We gonna kick ass and take names."

Barry and Slim pulled into a rest area and slept for several hours before checking the post office for instructions. Barry stayed in the sleeper, out of sight in case they might be watched. Slim climbed back in and rolled out on Highway 90.

When they were outside Van Horn, Barry climbed back into his seat. Slim handed him the letter. Barry read it and handed it back. "Short and to the point, Slim."

"Yeah. Now it gets dangerous, Barry. We're gonna be sittin' ducks out there at that roadside park. And I'm gonna tell you something: There ain't *nothin'* between Marathon and Sanderson except miles and miles of nothin'."

"So if they smell anything out of the ordinary, they'll kill us and split?"

"You got that right."

"Pickup truck coming up behind us," Barry said, checking the mirror.

"Might be one of our contacts. You better get in the sleeper, Barry."

Barry had just hit the bunk when the CB squawked. "Any word on how it's lookin' up ahead?"

"Ain't heard a peep," Slim radioed back.

"You mind if I stay in the rockin' chair?" the driver of the pickup asked.

"Not a bit."

"What's your handle?"

"Slim."

"I'm T-Bone."

"That's our contact," Slim called over his shoulder. "Stay out of sight, Barry. I'm goin' to 39."

He moved to channel 39 and pulled out the mike jack, inserting another.

"Scrambler mike?" Barry asked.

"Right. This ain't no two-bit outfit, Barry. Guy who runs it is connected pretty well with the government."

"Yeah," Barry said bitterly. "I know him."

"No shit? Well, you don't know much of a man. He likes

the little Mexican girls. Jack Morris is one sorry son of a bitch.''

"I'm finding that out. How little a girl does he like?"

"Real young." He spat out the window in disgust. "I don't understand that type of man."

"He isn't a man. He's a . . ." Barry paused. "I don't know what he is. Sorry is too good a word for him."

"I heard that. Lemme jaw with this dude, find out what's goin' down.

"I'm set," Slim radioed.

"Any trouble?"

"None at all. Everything smooth so far. You expectin' any trouble?"

"Maybe," the voice radioed back. "Did you know you stayed at the same motel with those SSTs from Rivers Trucking?"

"Yeah. I seen 'em. They broke regs and pulled out around midnight." Slim held up one hand and crossed his fingers for luck.

"That jibes with what I heard. But Rivers is no dummy. The boss says he's figured some of it out. But Rivers is in for a surprise. I don't know what kind of surprise, but I bet you it involves that blonde broad he married."

Slim looked over his shoulder, his face mirroring his shock and panic.

Barry felt a sickness in his guts. He motioned for Slim to continue talking.

"Yeah?" Slim said. "Well, that's her problem. I just don't want her problem to become *my* problem. You know what I mean?"

"I heard that. Well, we got time to get clear of the state before it goes down. Whatever it is that's going down."

"Gonna happen in Texas," Slim said to Barry. He keyed

his mike. "How could Rivers give us any trouble? He's clear up in Washington State."

"I don't know. The boss don't tell me everything, man. OK, Slim, I'm clear. I'll see you next run. Have a good one."

Slim watched as the pickup slowed, pulled over on the shoulder, and turned around, heading back toward Van Horn.

Barry slipped into his seat just as the sun was sinking toward dusk. "I gather there were code words you could have used if you were in trouble?"

"Right. Everything's all right. Barry, you got to call your people; warn them that they're due for some trouble."

"How, Slim? Beer Butt's taking my place. He'll be in the sleeper while they load. The others will tell the guards I've got the flu, the contagious kind, and to stay away. I call up there and someone's liable to smell a rat."

"Shit!" Slim summed it up.

Barry checked his map. "We'll be at the pickup point in about three and a half hours."

"Yeah. If we don't get behind some Sunday driver. But we might have to sit there and wait for two, three hours." He changed out the scrambler mike for the original, and normal CB chatter resumed.

Both men perked up their ears.

"Hey, Montana!" a voice called. "You got your ears on?"

"Speak to me, Shiny Hiney."

"Dolittle called in 'bout ten minutes ago. Damn near blowed my doors off with that jacked-up radio of his. He's settin' on ready."

"Good. I seen the Christmas tree. He's runnin' ahead of me."

"What's he talking about?" Barry asked.

"Me," Slim said with a grin. "He's talkin' about all my runnin' lights. You got some friends down here, Barry."

A Kenworth roared past Slim's Peterbilt. The driver grinned hugely, lifted a thumb in a gesture of "everything's all right," then picked up a shotgun from the seat beside him, holding it up so Slim and Barry could see.

"Well, I'll just be goddamned!" Slim said. "That's ol' Horsefly. Horsefly and Dolittle and Shiny Hiney and Montana's all good friends of Panty Snatcher. He musta called them."

A feeling of warmth that Barry had not experienced since his A-Team days in Asia washed over him. But he had to say, "Slim, do they know what they might be heading into?"

"Yeah, they know," Slim said, his voice soft, just audible over the roar of the engine and wind. "In the short time you've been back behind a wheel, Barry, you've made some good friends on the road."

"Crazy bastards," Barry said, speaking around the growing lump in his throat. "They could get *killed!*"

"They know it." Slim picked up his mike. "This is Christmas Tree. You boys copy?"

They did.

"You got Dolittle up east?"

"Ten-four."

"Warn him to stay clear of the pickup point. Stay east of it until he gets the word to come on in."

"Four on that, Christmas Tree. You still got that booster on your squawk box?"

"Ten-four," Slim radioed.

"We'll lay back eight or ten miles east and west of the pickup point. Holler when you want us to come in."

"Ten-four."

The air went silent.

"Those are good ol' boys," Slim said. "All combat vets from Korea. And they ain't got nothin' to lose, Barry. The bank is fixin' to take their rigs."

"They can lose their *lives*, Slim."

"Barry, they're about to lose their livelihood. Those ol' boys been truckers all their adult life. They don't know nothin' else. They're all around fifty years old. Man reaches fifty, it's kinda hard to find a job, of any kind. Truckers have their pride."

"Well, Slim, there is one company who'll hire them."

"Oh, yeah? What company is that?"

"Mine."

Slim's smile was sad. "You're forgetting something, Barry. Even if you get out of this alive, you're gonna be a wanted man. You're gonna have more warrants out on you than Jesse James."

The idea that had been forming in Barry's head began firming up. "Rivers Trucking will continue to function, Slim."

Slim glanced at him. "What in hell are you smiling about, Barry? You smilin' like a big tiger."

"That may be a very apt description, Slim. Much more than you know."

25

They had stopped at a cafe in Marathon where Slim had refilled thermos bottles with coffee and picked up a sackful of sandwiches. They pulled into the roadside park about thirty minutes later. They waited.

"Jesus!" Slim said. "What time is it?"

"About five minutes later than the last time you asked," Barry told him. He glanced at his wristwatch. "Coming up to midnight. The witching time of night."

"The *what* kind of night?"

"Shakespeare, Slim. ' 'Tis now the very witching time of night, When churchyards yawn, and hell itself breathes out contagion to this world.' "

"No shit!" Slim said. "All the same to you, I'll stick with Waylon. I had enough of Mr. Shakespeare in high school."

"Where was that?"

"Little town in Illinois. I left there when I was—"

The CB, set on 39, clicked twice.

Slim keyed his mike three times in response.

"Everything look good?" came the question out of the night air.

"Everything's fine," Slim spoke into his mike. "What's your ten-twenty?"

"About thirty miles out. Get ready."

"We'll be set."

Barry slipped out of the bunk and picked up his Uzi, belting ammo pouches around his waist. "I'll be around, Slim. Watch your ass."

Slim nodded and changed the CB channel to 19. He picked up his mike. "Thirty minutes to the DZ," he said.

"Green light on," came the response.

Barry said, "You an ex-jumper, Slim?"

"Eighty-Second Airborne. Korea. Montana was in the 101st. Shiny Hiney and Horsefly was Marine Raiders. Dolittle was UDT. We'll stand with you, Barry. Now get gone."

Barry climbed down into the inky darkness of midnight. Slim's voice stopped him just as he was closing the door.

"Barry? Thanks for givin' me a chance to redeem myself."

"Kissy, kissy!" Barry whispered.

"Asshole!" Slim laughed.

Barry lay beneath one of the tables in the roadside park. His heartbeat had picked up slightly, but his palms were dry as they gripped the Uzi. He had left his shotgun in the tractor with Slim. Barry forced all thoughts of Kate out of his head and concentrated on the upcoming unknown. He had no way of knowing how many men they might be facing. He and Slim knew only that a load of human beings were to be off-loaded for a run up to the Colorado experiment station.

And that atrocity must not be allowed to happen.

Barry waited.

* * *

Paul Rivers lay beside his wife in Baton Rouge. She was deep in sleep. He had not been able to keep his eyes closed. At first, when Jack approached him with his scheme, he had felt . . . well, *gritty* about it. He hadn't felt any emotion about his father being beaten by those . . . whoever it was Jack had hired to beat the old man.

A good thrashing was one thing—murder was quite another. Then he'd learned that his father had thrown in with that filth Fabrello. Bulgari was nothing more than educated slime. Paul was glad the mobster was dead.

More money for those remaining.

Paul's brother? . . . That had been, at first, thorny. But as time went by, the upcoming pill had not been all that difficult to swallow.

Especially after he learned his brother had actually *married* some woman truck driver. Some roadside whore, certainly. Everybody knew that truck drivers were trash, and the women even worse. For his brother to *marry* one of those repulsive creatures was beyond the comprehension of an intelligent person.

The others? Well, what was done was done. The wheels were in motion, and Paul could not stop it at this late date. His brother's ex-wife? . . . There would be no loss there. Paul had never really known her, and he supposed that made it easier.

His sister? . . . He had not seen her in years. He had never felt himself a part of the family.

Paul wondered, lying in bed, staring up at the ceiling, if he was insane.

Or just callous and greedy.

Perhaps a combination of all three.

* * *

In his Maryland apartment, Jack Morris fondled himself and thought of the young Mexican girls coming across the border on this run. He had instructed his field people to make certain there were several of them this trip. He liked to listen to them scream.

He suppressed a groan and fought back his growing erection.

He thought of the future. Looked very bright for him. Very rosy indeed.

He looked at his wife, sleeping beside him. He hated her. Goddamned drug addict. Well, when the next few days were past, he would think about disposing of her, too. An overdose would be the logical method, but that might draw too much heat on him. He could arrange an accident later on. Hell, he'd lived with her all these years, a few months more wouldn't make that much difference.

But first things must come first. And right this moment, Barry Rivers was at the top of the list.

With Barry out of the picture, troubled waters would smooth into calm seas. If he could stay with the cocaine business just a year more, he'd be worth millions; then he could back out of the business of helping supply live bodies to those experiment stations. He'd found it repulsive at first, but that was before he'd seen those young girls, and seen the endless possibility of smooth, young female children . . . to do with as he wished.

Barry's brother would be no problem; Jack knew he could handle that one. The man was nothing more than a hypocritical, greedy fool. And quite possibly insane.

Jack felt it would not take much to push him over the edge.

Well, he thought, closing his eyes, it would all be over

in two days. Kate would meet with a very unfortunate accident. In his grief, Barry Rivers would take his own life.
Donna would have an accident driving to New Orleans for
the funeral of her brother. What a pity. Terrible thing.
The children of Barry, of course, would remain unscathed.
It had taken some doing, but Jack had finally convinced
Paul of the necessity of that. He, Jack, out of the goodness
of his heart, would set aside a very large portion of the
business, the profits going directly into a special account
for the kids; a nice interest-bearing account. They, and the
widow, would be well taken care of.

And—Jack smiled in the gloom of his bedroom—that
would take any suspicion off him.

Yes, he thought, it looked good. Nothing was ever perfect, of course, but this was very close to perfection.

He slipped into sleep, a smile on his lips.

Barry watched as headlights topped the small rise from
the east. He could see the closed van behind the tractor.
Even with the vents open, it must be terribly hot inside,
he thought.

The rig pulled into the roadside park area and quickly
cut its lights. Using the sudden darkness, and knowing the
driver would have absolutely no night vision for several
minutes, Barry slipped from his concealment and ran
toward the new arrival. He slipped under the trailer and
waited.

"Utah Slim?" a man's voice called.

"Yeah," Slim answered. "You got a word for me?"

"Roundup."

"That's good. Where's your runnin' buddies?"

"Over that rise yonder. Lemme talk at 'em and tell 'em
to come on."

"You do that."

The driver radioed in and stepped out of the cab. He stepped out just in time to catch the balled fist of Barry on the back of his neck. The man slumped to the still-hot ground and lay still.

"Damn, Barry," Slim said. "I think you killed him."

Barry squatted down and jerked up the man's cowboy hat, plopping it on his head. "You care?"

"Not really." Barry could feel the man's eyes on him in the night. "You play rough, don't you, Barry?"

"I damn sure do, Slim. We don't have much time, so get cracking."

Slim quickly backed his rig up to the back doors of the trailer. He got out and walked between the trailers, speaking in rough border Spanish.

"*Sí,*" a man's voice came weakly. "*Bueno.*"

"They have to be in very bad shape," Barry said.

"I've seen half of them dead, partner," Slim said gruffly. "Goddammit, you can't blame the poor bastards for wanting to better themselves. You just can't."

"Tell them to get out of there and into your rig. And to stay put when the shooting starts."

"I'll tell 'em, but there ain't no way they're gonna do it," Slim said. "They gonna fly like rabbits."

"Tell them anyway. We can always hope."

The message delivered, Slim opened the back of his trailer just as headlights came at them from several directions.

"That ain't Frank!" both men heard someone yell. "Goddammit, what's going on?"

"Here comes the troops!" Slim said.

Both men heard the roaring of powerful engines. Barry lifted the Uzi and pulled the trigger, holding it back, spraying the nearest car with lead. Slugs pocked the windshield and sparked off metal as screams filled the Texas night.

"Close your trailer!" Barry shouted, ejecting the empty clip and slamming home a fresh one.

Slim slammed the doors, only slightly covering the screams of the panicked men and women and children inside.

"Tell them to get on the floor and stay there," Barry said.

"Descolgar! Acostarse!" He looked at Barry. "I think I got that right."

A yell ripped the night just after a rig slewed to a sliding halt, blocking the highway from the west. "The Marines is here, boys!" Shiny Hiney jumped down, a shotgun in his hands.

The yammering of a MAC-10 split the night, the slugs chopping up the ground in front of Shiny Hiney.

"Fuck the Marines!" a hoarse voice shouted from beside a four-wheeler.

Shiney lifted his shotgun and began squeezing and pumping, the magnun-pushed slugs ripping through the night, tearing great sparking holes in the car and sending two men flopping to the earth.

"Fuck the Marines, huh, you son of a bitch!" Shiny yelled, reloading. "You'll pay for that remark, damn you."

From the east, Horsefly's rig roared to a rubber-burning halt, blocking the way out. Horsefly jumped out, a Mini-14 with a thirty-round clip in his hands.

"Them sons of bitches is bad-mouthin' the Marines, Horsefly!" Shiny yelled. "Charge!"

"These sons of bitches are crazy!" a strange voice yelled. "Shit on this!" He tooked off running into the black vastness of Texas night, his heels kicking up little pockets of dust and sand as he galloped out of sight.

"Come back here, Jerry!" a man screamed.

"Screw you," Jerry called.

The man lifted a rifle and shot Jerry in the back. Jerry fell headfirst onto the ground and lay still.

"Nice folks," Barry said.

"Yeah," Slim said. He lifted a pistol and shot the man in the belly.

"I never knowed you could shoot like that, Slim," Shiny panted, nearly out of breath.

Slim looked at him and grinned. "As usual, the Paratroopers was here first."

"That's low, Slim," Shiny said. "That's real low."

Then everybody hit the dirt as lead started flying from all directions.

26

"Fire!" Barry shouted, cutting loose with his Uzi, knocking two men sprawling to the ground.

"Bossy bastard, ain't he?" Shiny said.

"I'd do what he says if I was you," Slim told him.

Hard gunfire cut the night as several of the peddlers of human flesh ran into the darkness, fleeing the firepower of the truck drivers.

Many people, unfamiliar with combat situations, or from watching too much garbage on the tube, never really know how it ends. Most of the time it doesn't taper off. It just stops.

The night was very quiet, very still. A silent shooting star cut the heavens with a silver plume. Gracefully fading away.

Slim looked up, following the star. "Maybe I done something right for a change," he said.

" 'Bout damn time," Dolittle called from beyond the

western perimeter. "If you'd got any worse I'd been forced to shoot you myself."

"There is truth in what he says," Slim admitted.

Montana joined the crowd, half-dragging, half-leading a man. "This one just got a little burn on the head," he said. "What do you wanna do with him?"

"I want a lawyer!" the man said.

"Hogtie him and put him in the trailer," Barry said. "We gotta get out of here. I'm surprised a car hasn't come along."

"I got my constitutional rights, man!" the flesh-peddler said. "I want my rights."

Barry turned and hit him flush on the side of the jaw, in front of his ear. The man dropped to the ground, out cold.

"Good right cross," Horsefly said.

A wounded man moaned, his cry of pain drifting through the gunsmoke-filled night. "Help me, somebody."

Barry thought of the mangled heads of the veterans; the doped-up and sexually abused women the guard had bragged about; the young children raped; the bits and pieces of dogs and cats. "Anybody volunteer to help him?" he asked.

No one did.

The truckers rolled out, heading east. Barry did not know what to do with the Mexicans.

"We gotta get rid of them, Barry." Slim broke into his thoughts. "I ain't tryin' to be hard or nothin', just practical."

"I know. But where?"

"Border patrol. Maybe their own people scattered around here. Unless you wanna go to the cops, that is?"

Both men knew, as Caesar did, that the die had been cast for them. There was no turning back.

"Stop at the next town," Barry said. "I'll make a phone call."

It had to be one of the most frustrating phone conversations Barry had ever endured.

"Barry," John Weston patiently explained, for the second time, "you have no proof they were being trucked to any experiment station. The Mexicans themselves didn't know *where* they were being taken, except across the border. Their testimony won't be worth spit. I wish to God you had contacted me before you went off half-cocked."

"Sure, John." Barry's reply was acid-tinged. "Some federal judge on the take, probably involved up to his or her ass in this slime, signed a search warrant against me. Every agency in D.C. has maverick agents within their ranks. Could you have guaranteed this would remain quiet?"

"No," John said with a sigh. "Barry, if you continue with this . . . wild scheme of yours, I'll probably be coming to arrest *you*. Can't I get that through your head?"

"How about the gunplay tonight?"

"I didn't hear that question, and don't repeat it."

"All right. What about my partner?"

"A paragon of virtue and straightforwardness. Nothing comes through his home or business phones. I've got them bugged. He does make some calls from various pay phones around town, but never the same one twice. He's smart, Barry."

"My brother?"

"Your brother is insane. Did you know he's been seeking professional help for years?"

220   *William W. Johnstone*

"No, I didn't. But it doesn't surprise me. He's weak, John; you could crack him."

"There again, we have this problem with warrants."

"Goddammit, John!" Barry flared. "What in the hell ever happened to the rights of law-abiding citizens?"

"Many of them got flushed down the toilet, pal. Now, about the Mexicans . . . Turn them loose, Barry."

"What?"

"Open the trailer doors and turn them loose. The local law will toss them in the clink, and within twenty-four hours, the Border Patrol will have them back in Mexico."

"Goddammit, John . . . there are *kids* here."

"I know, Barry. Far better than you do. It's sad and sick and disgusting and . . . a lot of other things. They'll be taken care of; fed, housed, and so forth. You can't do that. And they'll probably be back across the border into the U.S. within the week. If it takes them that long."

"Heading for another experiment station?" The question was bitter-sounding.

"There is always that possibility, Barry. Of all the people in the world, pal, you should know it's tough out there."

"Thanks, John. I needed that. What about the experiment stations? What have you found out?"

"You're not going to like this."

"I can believe that."

"Untouchable, buddy."

Barry was silent for a moment. "Would you mind explaining that?"

"There is a little-known but very, very powerful office in D.C. It's called the Center for Special Studies. CSS. Not to be confused with one that sounds similar. The CSS receives both government and private money. Believe it or not, and you probably won't, they've done some good work in the research field."

"What kind of research?"

The FBI man sighed. "I don't know, Barry. And I can't pry anymore. I've been ordered to back off and stand clear."

"By whom?"

"You do not have a need to know."

There it was. That same old very familiar bullshit Barry had heard so often in government quarters. *The need to know.* It should be renamed CYA. Cover Your Ass.

"John, those places are hellholes. They're carving up human beings. Women are being raped. Men and women are being fed massive amounts of dope and left to die. Animals are being mutilated—*alive.* Pets, John. Domestic animals. Dogs and cats. Men and women are being tortured, mentally and physically. And you're telling me you can't do one *fucking thing!*" he shouted.

"I'm afraid I'm going to have to terminate this conversation, Barry."

"John, my partner is up to his ass in dope and murder. My brother had our father beaten. There are contracts out on my wife's life, my father's life, my sister's life, the lives of my kids, and you're sitting up there in D.C. on your officious ass and telling me you—"

Barry stopped. He turned around, looking at Slim.

"What's wrong?" Slim asked.

"The son of a bitch hung up on me!"

Barry and Slim turned the Mexicans loose. It nearly broke Barry's heart to see the sad eyes of the little children, looking up at him.

Slim summed it up. "They can hang a guilt trip on you without even sayin' a word. Believe me, I know."

Barry imagined the man did, too. But Slim would have

to work out or live with his own personal demons. He dug in his jeans and handed the man he assumed to be the leader a wad of money.

"Let's go," he told Slim.

They were in Fort Stockton before dawn. There, Barry called his dad in New Orleans. "Rivers Trucking just hired four new drivers," he informed his father.

"Is that a fact?"

"Yes. They have their own rigs, too."

"Isn't that nice? Something tells me the company is going to have to come up with some money for back payments on those rigs, too."

"Yep."

"You're the boss," Big Joe said. But Barry could tell by his father's tone of voice the man was pleased with what he'd done.

"Gotta go, Dad. You take care."

He hung up before his father could say anything. He turned to the Texas drivers. "You guys heard it. Deadhead it to New Orleans. You have jobs waiting for you."

"What about you and Slim?" Dolittle asked.

"It would probably be better if you didn't know anything about that."

"Mr. Rivers," Horsefly said. "We'd rather stay with y'all."

"And get tossed in prison? Listen to me, right now, believe it, there are open warrants out on the people who left those dead and wounded by that roadside park. That's us, people. Now you guys take off for New Orleans."

"Better give us the number of the terminal in case we need to call in," Montana said, after sneaking a furtive look at Shiny. A look that Barry missed. He wrote down the number and the men all shook hands.

"We'll see y'all around," Dolittle said innocently.

"Yeah, take care, now," Horsefly said.

After Barry and Slim had pulled out, Montana said, "Now I call Big Joe Rivers. We got to look after them two crazies."

Jack Morris slowly replaced the phone into its cradle. He walked out of the office building and onto the busy streets of downtown Washington, D.C. His thoughts were as dark as a hidden cave.

Somebody, and Jack damn sure knew who that somebody was, had intercepted the transport of greasers and ambushed his men, turning the greasers loose.

God*damn* Barry Rivers.

He walked into the park and sat down. The Green Beret bastard had somehow organized a bunch of redneck truck drivers and shot up the place. Most of Jack's men, of the Texas contingent, were dead. Well, his spirits lifted a tad— that much was good. None of them would be talking. But two were still left alive, and that might present a problem. Not that he could be directly connected with anything; he was sure of that. He just didn't like loose ends flapping about.

He rose from the bench and walked to a pay phone. When his party came on the line, Jack said, "Kill the old man and anybody else who gets in your way."

"Let's spell it out," the voice said. "Big Joe Rivers dies?"

"Yes."

Jack hung up.

27

Barry and Slim took a state highway north out of Fort Stockton. About twenty miles out of town, they pulled over and parked by the side of an old barn. The ruins of a ranch house stood starkly vacant, mute in a deserted silence.

"Reckon why they left here?" Slim asked.

"A dream died," Barry said, opening the doors to the trailer.

"That's spooky, man. You sure you're not a poet, or something like that?"

"I'm sure." Barry dragged the flesh-peddler out and dumped him on the ground.

The man glared up at Slim. "They'll get you, Slim. You nothin' but a walkin'-around dead man."

"Maybe," Slim said. "But my hands are clean for the first time in a long time. It feels good, Sam. Believe me."

Sam spat on Slim's boots.

Barry knelt down beside the hogtied man. "We can do this easy, or we can do it hard, Sam. It's all up to you."

"I ain't tellin' you nothin', *prick!*" Sam blustered.

Barry's smile was savage, a brutal curving of the lips that held no semblance of mirth. "Yeah, you'll tell me, Sam."

"I don't think I wanna see this," Slim said.

"You probably don't." Barry's reply was softly spoken. He reached for Sam.

Sam was dead. His cooling body lay on the hot Texas sands. His face was contorted from that last moment of pain before his heart quit on him.

Slim had walked to the scene only once, leaving much faster than he arrived. He had puked on the ground and not looked back.

But Sam had talked. Slowly, with pain-filled words, he had told it all. The entire slimy, depraved, perverted tale.

Then he had cursed Barry with his last breaths and died.

"I don't ever want you for an enemy, Barry Rivers," Slim said, looking at the bloody sands.

Barry rose from his squat and stretched. "The VC had fifty thousand dollars on my head in 'Nam, Slim. A lot of them tried to collect it."

"Too bad we didn't have four, five more guys like you over there," Slim said dryly. "We'd have won the damn war."

Barry folded his lock-back knife and put it in the case on his belt. "You ready to go to war, Slim?"

"Might as well. What are we gonna do with Sam?"

"Leave him for the coyotes and the buzzards. And hope they don't get sick."

Standing by the truck, Barry opened his atlas and pointed at a spot just north of the Apache Mountains.

"One of the CSS experiment stations is located there. We're going to destroy it."

"All by ourselves?"

"You got a better idea?"

"Put this on my tombstone, Barry: He teamed up with a mighty mean man."

Laughing, Barry waved Slim into the truck.

"You got 'em in sight, Montana?" Horsefly asked over the CB.

"Four on that. Looks like they're gonna make it to Monahans and then take the interstate. But I don't know which way."

"Five'll get you ten it's west. Big Foot sent word the SSTs would be haulin' to just south of the Delawares. It's a goddamn setup, boys. We can keep trackin' 'em on the radio. You get in touch with Woodchuck, Dolittle?"

"Four on that. Him and Big Foot and Hawkeye are rollin' south right now. They're runnin' with the SSTs."

"Let's go, boys. Big Joe asked us to look out for his son, and that's what we're gonna do."

"I don't think that ol' boy *needs* no one to look after him. Four?"

"Be fun keepin' up with him and Slim, though," Shiny Hiney said.

"Some people think it's fun to play with rattlesnakes, too," Horsefly offered.

"We're workin' for the man." Montana settled it. "Big Joe is wirin' the money to our banks. Our rigs is OK, our families secure. My grandaddy rode for the King Ranch. His daddy with Goodnight. You take the man's money, you ride for the brand."

"Before you bring us all to the point of tears with this

sad tale of yours," Horsefly said, "why don't you just grab hold of that gearshift and put the pedal to the metal and roll?"

"I'm tryin' to educate you ignorant bastards," Montana radioed.

"Only person in the history of education to ever flunk recess, and he's gonna teach us," Dolittle said.

"I give up," Montana said disgustedly.

"Good!" the others all radioed.

"I got a bad feelin' in my guts," Beer Butt told Kate.

"Such as?" the little blonde asked, behind the wheel of the Kenworth as they approached the New Mexico border.

"It's comin' down to the wire, Kate. I wish to God you'd reconsider and hunt a safe spot and stay put."

"We been over that, Beer Butt. No dice. I'm staying."

The big man signed. "I knew that's what you'd say. Turn off right up here. Get on that state road."

"Beer Butt . . . if something bad is going to happen, I want to be with my man."

"I understand." He spoke gently. He reached for their logbook and looked at it. "Christ, what a mess. If we wasn't pullin' SSTs the ICC would ground us."

"How far are we from the cutoff?"

" 'Bout three hours, Kate. He's all right, girl. If something had happened to him, we'd have heard on the CB."

"You know damn well he was involved in that shootout we heard about. He might be hurt."

"I doubt it. Barry Rivers is one randy bastard. We'd have heard."

"Beer Butt?"

"Yes, Kate."

"How come people think truck drivers are stupid? We're

not hauling electronic gear for fighter planes. Listen to that damn stuff rattle, would you?''

"I know.''

"They're using us to get to Barry, aren't they?''

"That's the way I see it, Kate. And with us dead, whoever takes over the company will put their own drivers in. The government contract will remain in force. From then on, it'll be smooth sailin'. They can haul dope or human beings, or whatever they choose to haul. And nobody will question it. It's big, Kate. A whole lot bigger than Barry first thought.''

"But first they've got to get rid of us, right?''

"Yep.''

"They'd better send some damn rough ol' boys to do that,'' she said grimly.

Beer Butt looked at her and grinned. TNT was right, he thought.

Barry drove right up to the gates of the CSS station and honked his horns. And honked.

A guard finally stepped out of the air-conditioned blockhouse and looked through the wire at the Peterbilt. "What the hell do you want?'' he yelled.

"How do you like living?'' Barry asked, sticking his head out the window.

"Beg pardon?''

"You heard me.''

Slim jacked back the hammer on his pistol.

"You better carry your ass on away from here, boy,'' the guard said. "Just back that big bastard up and haul it!''

Barry dropped the Peterbilt into gear and rammed the gates. The guard squalled and cussed as he jumped out of the way. Barry stopped and Slim stuck his pistol out the window.

"Drop your gun belt and start runnin'. Don't look back. Just keep on goin'. Things are about to get hot around here."

"You guys are crazy!" the guard yelled.

Slim put one round between the guard's feet. The guard jumped and dropped his gun belt. "Now run, boy!" Slim yelled.

The guard ran, running as if demons were pursuing him. He did not look back.

"What's the plan, Barry?" Slim asked.

"What plan?" Barry said with a grin. "Just bear this in mind, Slim: there are no innocent people working in this hellhole."

"We go in shootin'?"

"Just like John Wayne."

"Hammer down, Barry Rivers."

The compound was rapidly filling with people, some of them with guns in their hands, all of them pointed at Barry and Slim.

Barry gunned the engine and spun the wheel hard left, the empty trailer sliding on the pea gravel of the compound. The rig was in no danger of overturning, but to the inexperienced eyes of the civilians, it appeared the long trailer was about to fall over and crush them.

They panicked, running in all directions, many of them screaming and yelling in fright.

"Shoot those sons of bitches!" a white-coated man yelled, pointing at the Peterbilt.

"That's my cue," Slim said. He put a .38 round at the man's feet and the man jumped about a foot off the ground, hollering. He came back to earth and fell down on the pea gravel, scooting and crawling behind a bush. His head was protected but his ass was sticking out.

"Wish I had me a shotgun with bird shot in it," Slim said with a grin.

A slug whined wickedly through the windshield, causing both men to cringe and duck. Barry lifted the Uzi and put a few 9mm rounds over the head of the gunman. The guard dropped his service revolver and took off running.

"So much for experienced guards," Barry muttered, opening his door. "Most of these people are unarmed, Slim. Let's round 'em up."

"When in doubt, charge!"

"That's it."

Both men jumped from the truck, Barry to the left, Slim to the right. They zigzagged their way through the running, milling-about, and frightened people, shoving and pushing them toward what Barry guessed was an office building. All the fight seemed to have gone out of the guards. Like so many untrained, gun-toting civilian guards, when it came down to the nut-cuttin', their inexperience overrode bluster and they quit.

The director of this particular hellhole finally realized his ass was sticking out past the bush and got to his feet, his face red and his hands trembling. He faced Barry and Slim.

"I'll have the law on you!" he yelled.

Barry slapped him, rocking the man's head back and bloodying his mouth. "Shut up until you're told to speak."

"Now see here!" the man yelped.

Barry hit him with a hard, chopping right fist. The man dropped to the hot ground and covered his bloody and bruised mouth with his hands. He sobbed into his palms.

"Please don't hit him again," a woman spoke. "Haven't you hurt him enough?"

Barry turned to face her. "Lady—and I use the term loosely—unless you want to spend the next five years visiting plastic surgeons, I want the keys to the cells, or wards, or whatever you people call your lock-downs."

The woman could have been pretty, if she would soften her mouth and eyes. "You have to be Barry Rivers. You're a foolish man, Mr. Rivers. Like so many well-intentioned people—foolish."

"Spare me the rhetoric, lady. Just take me to the prisoners."

She arched one eyebrow. "We call them patients, Mr. Rivers."

"I doubt that many of them would agree with you," Barry replied. "Move your ass."

"Don't be crude," she said primly.

For a reply, Barry poked her in the belly with the barrel of the Uzi. "Move!"

She paled and nodded her head.

"Everybody on the ground!" Barry said, raising his voice. "On your bellies and keep your faces in the dirt." He glanced at Slim. "The first one to raise their head gets it blown off." The woman could not see his wink.

Slim nodded and stuck his .38 behind his belt. He pumped a round into the slug gun. "You got it, Barry."

"Move, lady," Barry told the woman.

The facility was worse than a hellhole. It looked like a Nazi concentration camp. The cells were filthy; the prisoners in even worse shape. Many of the men and women were naked, or very nearly so. Barry could see that most of them had been beaten, some of them many times, the marks of old beatings visible under fresh bruises.

"They have to be disciplined," the woman said. "For their own sake and safety."

Before Barry even realized he had done it, his hand flew

out and slapped the woman, staggering her, knocking her back against the wall.

"Hit her again," a man said, his voice weak, his words slurred.

Barry watched the woman slide to the floor, her lips leaking blood. She was stunned, her eyes glassy.

He turned to look at the man. Not a young man; perhaps in his early fifties. His eyes were deep-sunk, reminding Barry of photos he'd seen of Jews in Nazi prison camps. But the eyes, haunted as they were, possessed a high level of intelligence.

"How many can I safely turn loose?" Barry asked him.

"Not too many of them. Sadly, most here are suffering from varying degrees of mental illness. Most of them service-related."

"And you?"

He smiled. "I am one of the two hundred thousand or so people who vanish each year, for whatever reason. Did you know the number was that large, Mr. Rivers?"

"No, I didn't. And how in the hell do you know my name?"

"Perhaps you should ask our dear Miss Bradshaw, the darling of this facility. The one you just smacked in the mouth."

Barry looked down at the woman. Her eyes were clearing as the effects of the hard blow left her.

She met his eyes. "We were expecting you, Mr. Rivers. Unfortunately, our guards were not up to the situation. You may succeed in . . . well, interrupting operations at this facility, Mr. Rivers, but not for long. I think any good odds-maker would put your chances of living very low."

Barry stared at her until she was forced to shift her eyes away from his menacing gaze. She cursed as she lost the visual battle. "Son of a bitch," she ended it.

"For all her education, she does have quite a filthy mouth," the prisoner said.

"And you?" Barry looked at him.

"I have a Ph.D. In psychology," he added, his tone dry enough to effect a martini.

Barry jerked the keys from a belt around the woman's waist and unlocked the door. The man stepped out. "Free at last," he said. Then, smiling, he said, "Although my situation and Dr. King's are somewhat different."

Barry handed the man the keys. "Turn loose the ones you feel are capable of fending for themselves."

Taking the keys, the man said, "How do you know I'm not a vicious maniac?"

"I don't. But if you show any tendencies in that direction, I can always shoot you." He lifted the muzzle of the Uzi.

"I do get the point. Oh, my name is Charles Matthews. I've been here for only four months. But I'm afraid I do have a drug addition." He looked at Miss Bradshaw through eyes that held a mixture of hate and contempt. "Thanks to her and others of her ilk."

"When was your last fix?"

"Not long ago. I'll be all right for several hours. Mr. Rivers," he said, pointing, "beyond that door is a veritable chamber of horrors. Please do something for those poor animals."

"You'll watch her?" He pointed to the woman, still sitting on the floor.

'I would cheerfully kill her."

Barry walked to the door, opened it, and puked on the hall floor.

28

Wiping his mouth and taking several deep breaths, Barry glanced at Matthews. "Tell my partner I'm going to be doing some shooting in here, and not to be alarmed."

"But of course," Matthews said.

Barry slung his Uzi and pulled out his 9mm. He walked to a table where a Husky was strapped down, wires implanted in the animal's head. She had been cut open, and the incisions were badly infected. Her pain was mirrored in her eyes. Barry wondered why the animal was not whining in her horrible pain.

He turned and asked Miss Bradshaw.

"We operated on the bitch's throat, preventing her from making any sound. Hell, Rivers. It's just a *dog*."

"How long has she been like this?" Barry was doing his best to fight back a terrible, wild rage building deep within him.

Miss Bradshaw shrugged. "Several weeks. I'd have to consult the charts."

Barry stepped out into the hall and kicked the woman in the mouth with his boot. Her jaw splintered with a pop and her teeth bounced off the floor and walls. The woman's head banged off the wall behind her and she slumped to the floor, unconscious, her blood staining the tile.

Matthews said, "You cannot realize how much personal satisfaction that gives me."

Barry turned and reentered the torture chamber. He petted the Husky's head and said, "Easy, girl. It'll soon be over for you." He lifted the 9mm and ended the animal's suffering.

If dogs and cats have a heaven? . . . Barry thought.

He went to every cage and table, ending each particular animal's suffering—all for the sake of science, of course.

Barry was on the verge of tears when he left the so-called laboratory. What confronted him brought the tears flowing, unchecked even if he had wanted to stop the flow.

He leaned against the door and stared in utter disbelief.

Some of the men and women were half-starved, that in addition to the marks and scars of beatings. Others were clearly suffering the effects of prolonged drug addiction. The ones Matthews had released appeared normal enough—mentally speaking—but Barry knew nothing of what might be lying behind those eyes.

Miss Bradshaw moaned in her unconsciousness. Barry hoped she was experiencing a nightmare. But he doubted it.

He looked up at the sounds of boots in the hall. He was not surprised to see Montana, Shiny Hiney, Horsefly, and Dolittle.

"What is this goddamned place?" Montana asked, his voice hushed.

"A horror story," Barry told him. "If you want to know what kind of people we're dealing with, look at these men and women, and then look in there." He pointed to the laboratory.

The truckers looked in, pulled their heads out, and walked stiffly back outside. The sounds of their sickness drifted to Barry.

"Matthews," Barry said. "Some of you drag Miss Bradshaw out of here and dump her outside. Tell my partner to bring my camera and start shooting film of this place. Shiny?"

"Ho," Shiny called.

"Watch the folks on the ground."

"Done."

"What happens when I turn you people loose?" Barry asked Charles Matthews, standing in the open hall door.

"We try to pick up our lives, sir."

"Go to the police?"

"No. It would do no good. The people who run these places would just go further underground. It's government sanctioned, you know."

"Yes, I know," Barry said wearily.

"You mean our tax dollars are going to help support this . . . this *place*?" Montana asked.

"I'm afraid so. It's privately funded, as well. But this place is just about to be put out of business."

"What's gonna happen to it?"

"I don't know, yet." He watched as Slim, a grim look on his face, began taking pictures of the experiment station. He was visibly paler after leaving the laboratory.

"Person that would do that to a dog or cat oughta be tarred and feathered and then branded," Slim said. He walked on, pausing in front of each filthy cell, taking pictures with Barry's 35mm.

"Barry," Montana said, "these folks should be taken to a hospital. Some of them are in pretty rough shape."

"I know. But where, and how? The nearest town is about fifty miles away."

"Put them in my rig." Dolittle spoke from the doorway. His voice was choked with emotion. "I'll come up with some story as to how I got here."

"You're letting yourself in for a lot of grief," Barry reminded him.

Dolittle shrugged. "I wouldn't be able to live with myself if I didn't do it."

Charles Matthews walked back inside. Barry glanced at him. "Tell me this, Charles. Why? What is the point and purpose of this horror?"

"From what I was able to gather during my lucid moments, all types, or many types, of new, unproven drugs are tested here and in other places. How much pain the human body can endure before breaking. What the best method is to attack certain types of drug addiction. There is one facility, I don't know the location, where only work on the AIDS problem is done. Homeless people and illegal aliens are used because apparently nobody gives a damn what happens to them."

"Surely, surely, no one in the upper echelons of government sanctions places like these?"

"Oh, I wouldn't think so. The President probably knows of the CSS, but not what they really do behind closed doors. Unfortunately, I did find out. Pressure was applied on the hiring and firing committee of the institution where I used to teach. I was terminated. Blackballed. I have no family to speak of, so I was not really missed. Some men grabbed me one evening, right off the street, and eventu-

ally I was brought here. I will accompany your driver to
the nearest hospital, Mr. Rivers, but I must warn you of
this: these people, most of them, have been here for a
long, long time. They have all undergone mind-altering
procedures. Even if they did testify, no one would believe
a thing they had to say. Many of them can't track very
well, conversationally speaking. A few are no more than
gibbering idiots. Many are very close to that point." He
paused, his brow wrinkling in deep thought.

"What are you trying to say, Charles?" Barry asked.

"I'm assuming you know the location of all the experiment stations."

"I do."

"Then you have to destroy them, Mr. Rivers. Or as many
as humanly possible. For humanity's sake."

"I agree, Charles. But we have some obstacles in our
way, and I think you know what I'm talking about."

"The personnel assigned to this place. Yes. You don't
have to worry about the guards. They're nothing more
than thugs and drifters. No decent person would consider
working in such a place. They've run away, and they won't
talk or return. I'll bet on that. They fear prosecution. It's
the others. I haven't a clue as to what to do with them."

"Did the people who run these . . . torture chambers
really think their existing guards would be able to stop
me, or whatever they had in mind for me?"

Charles shrugged. "I suppose. Being one of the inmates,
I was not privy to that type of information."

Barry turned to Montana. "Help Dolittle get the people
loaded and get them out of here. Then bring the personnel
to me. I'll be in the main office building."

Charles stuck out his hand and Barry shook it. "See you
around, Charles."

"Thank you, Mr. Rivers."

* * *

"I don't know what in the hell I'm going to do with you people," Barry told the small gathering of so-called doctors and administrators and technicians. "I ought to just shoot you and be done with it."

Miss Bradshaw lay on a couch, her broken jaw and busted mouth swelling grotesquely. She managed a squeal of fright at that prospect. And it was genuine. She could attest to Barry Rivers's volatile temper.

"But I'm not going to do that," Barry said.

An audible sigh was heard.

"What I am going to do is this: You all will be provided with paper and pen. You will write out everything, *everything*, you know about what goes on in the various experiment stations around the country. You will name names, dates, and anything else you know. Who hired you, how you get paid, how many people you witnessed dying in these snake pits, how, and where they are buried—if they are buried. Get busy and don't fuck up, people. 'Cause I'll kill you if you do."

With the men and women writing frantically, Montana standing watch over them, Barry stepped outside just as the sounds of trucks reached his ears. As any trucker can attest, each rig sounds different, and Barry could hear his Kenworth rolling, Swamp Wolf's rig right behind it.

Kate swung down and into Barry's arms.

"Where's the rest of the crew?" Barry asked.

" 'Bout half an hour behind us," Kate said, looking up at Barry. "We off-loaded just outside El Paso, then were told to come here."

"Here?"

"Yeah," Swamp Wolf said. "This another one of them experiment stations?"

"Yes. I think we got troubles, people. I think we've just been set up."

Beer Butt looked out at the vastness of landscape that surrounded the station. Plumes of dust were kicked up high by fast-moving vehicles coming toward them.

"Montana!" Barry called. "Lock those people down and get out here. Grab your guns."

29

The station's personnel locked down in the main building, Montana had gathered up the hastily written and signed documents and given them to Barry. Barry stowed them in his Kenworth. The drivers turned their attention toward the half-dozen vehicles that had stopped just outside the complex gate, blocking the only road.

There were five men to a car, all heavily armed. One of the men held a cowboy hat in his hands. Barry recognized it. Dolittle had been wearing it when he pulled out for the nearest town with the sick and abused men and women . . . and Charles.

"Looks like we spoiled your party, Rivers," the man holding Dolittle's hat said.

"Maybe," Barry replied, the Uzi in his hand. "Where'd you get the hat?" Barry felt he knew how the hat had been obtained. But before he started wholesale killing, he wanted to know for sure.

"Took it off the head of a friend of yours, Rivers. He must have thought an awful lot of it. We had to kill him to get it."

Montana's knuckles turned white with strain as he gripped his shotgun.

"And the men and women he had with him?" Barry asked.

The man tossed the hat to the sands. "Nobody has to worry about them anymore."

"You are a sorry son of a bitch!" Montana cussed him.

The man laughed. "I think I'll just gut-shoot you, mister, and leave you for the ants to eat."

Montana lifted the muzzle of his shotgun and pulled the trigger, opening the dance. The buckshot tore half the man's face off and slammed him to the ground, his M-16 dropping from suddenly lifeless fingers.

The men from the four-wheelers had been bunched together when Montana lowered the boom with his shotgun. Beer Butt had edged to the left side of the compound, Swamp Wolf to the right side. They fired almost simultaneously, their shotguns roaring and belching flame and smoke and buckshot, the double-ought shot tearing great holes in the men. Five of the men were down before the others could fully recover and react.

Two of the attackers spun around and attempted to duck behind one of their cars. Barry gave them a short burst from the Uzi, the 9mm slugs catching them in the back and spilling them forward. They landed on their faces on the ground.

Kate was kneeling on the ground, by the rear of the trailer, working the twenty-gauge. She knocked a leg out from under one man, sending him to the hot sands screaming in pain, his leg bent and mangled under him as he fell, and put a load of magnum-pushed shot into another's belly. If he survived, he would be eating baby food for a long, long time.

The truckers were still badly outnumbered, but the surprise was still on their side, and they took advantage of it, keeping up the deadly hail of lead.

Shiny and Slim were on their bellies on the ground, both of them with M-16s taken from the experiment station's arms room. They were not being very hospitable toward the newcomers or their vehicles. Lead from one of the M-16s had set one car on fire, smoke boiling from under the hood. All knew it would not be long before the car's gas tank blew, and as bunched up as the attackers were, they would bear the brunt of the explosion.

"Fire at the gas tanks!" Barry yelled, his voice carrying over the din of battle. "Blow the bastards to hell!"

Montana suddenly grinned at Barry and jumped to his cowboy-booted feet, zigzagging toward his truck.

"Where you goin', you crazy freight-hauler?" Horsefly yelled.

"Cover him!" Barry yelled.

Montana made it to his truck and opened the outside storage compartment. All the drivers then knew what he was planning.

Red sticks began flying over the cab of the truck. Slim, Barry, and Beer Butt each caught one and looked at each other, grinning.

They were holding road flares.

The men sparked the flares into hot, sputtering flame and tossed them over the fence, toward the leaking gas tanks of the four-wheelers.

"Hit the ground!" Barry yelled.

The fumes ignited and the cars blew, sending pieces of hot metal and bits and chunks and globs of human flesh all over the nearby landscape.

Just as the remaining attackers were getting to their feet, stunned and confused by the blasts, Barry yelled, "Finish them!"

Shotguns and rifles and pistols blasted the still-shock-waved air, knocking the addled attackers to the sands, dead and dying.

"Cease fire!" Barry called. He had to call the order several times before the last weapon ceased cracking.

Inside the main office building, men and women were screaming in fright, begging for somebody to help them. They were smashing at windows, breaking the glass, but unable to get out because of the bars covering the windows. The front and back doors were all metal, impossible to smash through.

The building was blazing, set on fire from the flying bits of flame after the explosion.

The carpet and drapes and wooden paneling were blazing, sending out black clouds of choking smoke.

"Who has the keys to the building?" Barry asked.

Montana shrugged. "All I done was just close the front door," he said.

"They deserve whatever they're gettin'," Horsefly said. "Maybe it's justice. Them gettin' the first taste of Hell."

No one said anything out loud, but they all agreed with him . . . to a point.

"We better haul our asses outta here," Beer Butt said. "They's liable to be cops crawlin' all over this place pretty damn quick."

"Aw, shit!" Slim said. "I can't leave them sorry bastards and bitches in there. Goddammit, I just can't."

He ran to his Peterbilt and opened the outside storage compartment, dragging out a heavy chain, hooking one end to the rear of his trailer.

He looked at the others, the expression on his face silently telling it all.

"Well . . . crap!" Horsefly said. "Oh, all right!" He ran to Slim and grabbed the other end of the chain, running to a barred window, burning his hands as he looped the chain through the steel and secured it.

Beer Butt had raced to the Kenworth and grabbed another chain, hooking one end to the rear of Slim's Peterbilt and the other end to another barred window.

"Go!" Kate yelled to Slim.

Slim dropped the transmission into gear and rumbled forward, jerking the bars loose, in the process pulling out part of both front walls.

Burning men and women staggered out of the smoking, broken building, their clothing and hair on fire. They fell to the compound grounds, shrieking in the awful, burning pain.

"Jesus," Barry said. "Now what?"

"Trucks comin'," Beer Butt said.

Lady Lou was in the front truck, Beaver Buster behind the wheel.

Briefly, Barry explained what happened. Lou said, "You can see this smoke for miles. Won't be long before somebody sends help. I was a nurse before I got married. I'll stay, take care of these folks best I can. Y'all better get movin'. The guns in my rig is clean. The cops can't connect me with none of this. I'll tell 'em I don't know what happened; I just saw the smoke and pulled in here."

"We'll tell them," Beaver Buster corrected.

"Let's split!" Barry ordered.

Jack Morris could scarcely contain his rage upon hearing the news. After hearing the terse telephone message over his office phone, Jack left the office, telling his secretary he would not be back that day.

He drove aimlessly, attempting to cool his anger. That bastard Rivers was continuing to screw things up royally; was there no way he could be stopped?

The men sent to kill the old man hadn't even gotten within a half mile of him before Fabrello's men gunned them down and then vanished before the cops got there. Now Rivers and a handful of ragtag, ignorant truck drivers had wiped out—*totally*—a CSS experiment station *and* some of the best men Morris had working for him.

Jack knew, of course, that Barry was an expert when it came to fighting, but goddammit, no one man is invincible. Lucky, yes, but sooner or later luck has to run out.

Maybe, he mused, he should just take what he had gathered thus far, and cut and run?

That was certainly something to be considered.

But . . . no.

He had come this far, and he wasn't going to stop now, not until he had completed his initial plan.

Jack was a thief, sexually twisted, and totally amoral, but despite that, or because of it, he was no fool. He felt that by now, certainly, Barry knew he was involved in the operation. He had no idea how Barry might have found out, but he felt certain the man knew.

He whipped into a service station and placed a call to Paul Rivers. The man was badly shaken by the recent events. To Jack, he seemed confused and mentally disoriented. He babbled and ranted and could not keep a coherent train of conversation.

Jack finally hung up on the fool.

He dialed another number. No reply. Christ, his well-thought-out and -conceived network was falling apart.

He walked back to his car, wondering what Barry Rivers was up to now.

"Where are we headin', Barry?" Kate asked.

"Arizona. We'll link up with the rest of our gang and head out." He chanced a glance at her. "Kate, I'm about to become the most wanted man in America. I'm going to destroy as many of these damnable experiment stations as I can. I've had the word put on me by the federal people: either I quit, or they'll be coming after me. I'm not going to quit, Kate."

"I didn't figure you would," she said. "But before you start runnin' your mouth and stickin' your boot in it, hear this: I'm stayin'. With you. Beside you. All the way. And so are the others. They asked me to tell you that."

"I won't permit that, Kate. *Hear me out!*" he said, with more heat than he intended. "I've got to have friends on the road for my plan to succeed. The others will be no good to me if they're busy looking over their shoulders for the law. You see what I'm getting at?"

She was silent for many miles. During that time, the widely separated convoy met half a dozen police cars, lights flashing, sirens wailing, all headed, they guessed, for the source of the smoke still drifting into the air.

"Yes," Kate finally spoke. "Just don't include me in that plan to stay behind."

Barry knew there was no point in even talking about that. "All right," he reluctantly agreed. "But you'll do what I tell you to do, when I tell you to do it, without hesitation or question?"

"Yes," she said quietly.

"Louder, Kate."

"I said, ten-four, Rivers!" she shouted.

Barry grinned at her just as Jim Carson and the other drivers for Rivers Trucking showed up on the horizon. "Little but loud."

"And stubborn," she added.

Barry thought it best not to agree too much.

30

At a truck stop on Interstate 10, just outside Las Cruces, at a table set back from the other over-the-road drivers, Barry laid it all out for his people.

"If you think I'm gonna let Kate go ramblin' off into a firefight alone, you're crazy!" Beer Butt informed Barry. "There ain't no way you're gonna keep me out of this."

Coyote, Swamp Wolf, Cottonmouth, and Cajun agreed with Beer Butt. They were staying, come hell or high water.

Barry knew there was no point in arguing with the men. He glanced at the other drivers around the table. To a person they wanted to go, but their wives and kids were invisibly standing in their way.

Barry made it easier for the married men. "You people will continue to haul the contracted cargo in the SSTs. Rivers Trucking has got to make some money to keep my schemes going. Jim, you're the road boss. You call the shots for the others. You best put some distance between us and yourselves. You've got your traveling orders. Take off."

One by one, the drivers left. No one made a big show of shaking hands, not wanting to draw attention to anyone.

But the road has its own code; the only code long-distance haulers will answer to. And all the Rivers drivers knew there was not a driver in the cafe that didn't know who they were and what they were up to. Silently knew. And that silence would stay on the road.

The three wildcatters from the West Coast, Woodchuck, Big Foot, and Hawkeye, stayed at the table. Along with Montana, Cottonmouth, Cajun, Swamp Wolf, Horsefly, Coyote, Shiny, Slim, Barry, and Kate.

"Any of you boys married?" Barry asked.

They shook their heads.

"I been knowin' Dolittle since we was boys," Hawkeye said. "We grew up together," he added, his voice thick. He cleared his throat and stook a sip of coffee. "You couldn't get me away from this operation with a pry bar."

Barry looked at Big Foot, waiting until the waitress had poured them all fresh coffee and left. Someone slugged the jukebox; Narvel Felts was singing "One Run for the Roses."

Big Foot summed it up this way: "My home is the road, and I mean that literally. I sleep in motels and hotels and rest areas."

Vague, but Barry and the others understood. Barry glanced at Woodchuck.

Woodchuck said, "Oh, I'll just go along for the ride, I reckon. I always did like a good fight."

"Here it is," Barry said. "Me and Kate. Shiny and Beer Butt. Horsefly and Coyote. Swamp Wolf and Cajun. Cottonmouth and Montana. Slim and Hawkeye. Woodchuck and Big Foot. We're going to have to stock up with ammunition and other emergency gear. The money I wired for is in. So I'll tell you what I'm buying with it. Motorcycles.''

The truckers began grinning.

"A couple of dune buggies.''

The grins became wider.

Barry tossed some money on the table. "I know some of you boys can buy dynamite. Get as much as you can. Do it now. We'll all meet at the intersection of Interstates 8 and 17 tomorrow. We've all got boosters on our CBs. Stay on channel thirty-one. If we get separated after we bust up the facility in Arizona, head for Utah.'' He pointed to a spot on a Utah map. "Right there. Take some time out to check your wills. For a fact, some of us won't be coming out of this alive. I'm calling my attorney right now. I would suggest you all do the same.''

Barry rose from the table and walked to a bank of pay phones, dialing Ralph Martin's number back in D.C.

The news he heard was not good.

"Justice has the wheels in motion, Barry. There will be warrants out for you by the end of this week. Give it up. If you don't, you're tossing your career and future right out the window.''

Barry thought of the now-dead men and women he'd released from the Texas experiment station. He thought of the . . . he-didn't-know-how-many more scattered around the nation, tortured, drugged, raped. "I'm in this until the end, Ralph.''

"Then you're a goddamned fool.''

Barry didn't feel like arguing that with the man.

"What do you think you are, or have become, Barry? Some white knight in an eighteen-wheeler?''

"That's a good song, Ralph.''

"*What?*''

"The song.''

"You want to change your will, Barry?" Ralph's voice held a flat note.

"Everything to Kate. If we both go out, you have your instructions."

"I think I'll be talking with you very soon, Barry."

"Oh?"

"Yes. From some goddamned jail." He hung up.

When Barry returned to the table, Woodchuck and Big Foot were gone, along with Cottonmouth and Montana. Some of the money was gone with them.

The matter of explosives was being taken care of.

Shiny said, "I know an old boy who's got a fifty-caliber machine gun he'd like to get rid of." He looked at Barry. "You interested?"

"You know where the money is."

Shiny and Beer Butt left the table.

"I got a buddy in Tuscon runs a cycle shop," Hawkeye spoke. "He owes me a couple of real big favors. I think me and Slim will head thataway."

Barry signed some checks and handed them over.

Slim and Hawkeye left the table.

Horsefly's hands were coated with ointment and bandaged. His shifting hand was not as badly burned as his left hand. He could still drive. He said, "I know where I can get some stuff we'll probably need 'fore all this is over." He picked up the rest of the money from the table.

Horsefly and Coyote rose and walked out.

"Let's go, gang," Barry said.

"Goddamn fool!" Jackson said. "He's going to wind up in prison."

"Or dead," Stemke said.

John Weston said, "I think I can delay those warrants

until the first of next week. We'll let Barry dig his personal hole a bit deeper and then we'll have him."

"You're not serious!" Borman said.

Weston met the man's eyes, then shifted to touch every eye in the room. "You are all familiar with what the Cowboy who sits in Sugar Cube told us privately."

"That was no more than wistful thinking on his part," Jennings said.

"I don't think so. I'm going to meet with him tomorrow at Camp David. I think he's going to give me the green light."

"What's the latest body count out in Texas?" Borman asked.

"Twenty-three of Jack Morris's guns. Several of the station's personnel." His face tightened. "And all those poor bastards and bitches who were inmates there."

"I have never liked doing this to Barry," Jennings said. "We've lied to him, used him, set him up, and now we're sealing his future forever. I personally think it's shitty!"

Martin spoke for the first time. "Not to mention the other truckers who might come out of this alive. It's regrettable, but very opportune, wouldn't you all agree with that?"

"I still think this is storybook stuff," Jennings said. "Not to mention just as illegal as hell."

"But think what an edge it would give us in combatting crime." Weston argued his case. "One man, or a half a dozen, as the case may be, with tacit government approval, with every conventional weapon known to exist at his fingertips. A fully equipped eighteen-wheeler . . . an SST rig. With a new identity, no past record, able to travel anywhere within the Northern Hemisphere. That's it!" he said, excitement in his voice.

"What's it?" Jennings questioned, doubt edging the question.

"The SST bit. Hell, we'll have him actually carrying loads. He's working for the government anyway. Will be."

"*If* he agrees to go along with this crazy scheme." Borman dropped the other boot.

"Gentlemen," Weston said impatiently, "you're all forgetting one little item: Barry won't have any choice in the matter. It's either accept the proposal or go to prison on a multitude of charges. He's in a box, boys. And we're the only ones who can untie the string."

"What would be his limitations?" Stemke asked.

"That's the beauty of it all," Weston replied, leaning back in his chair and staring up at the ceiling. "No limits at all. The Dog would be judge, jury, and executioner. Justice would be in his hands."

"The *Dog*?" Borman asked.

"That's Barry's CB handle. It's almost poetic, boys. A snarling, foaming-at-the-mouth, fangs-bared Dog, on the side of the law, able to be unleashed at will, working for the law-abiding citizens of this nation, roaming the highways, for the most part, picking his targets at his own choosing. Be kind of nice if he had a dog with him," Weston muttered.

"Jesus, Weston!" Jackson said. "Don't get carried away."

"Oh, Barry!" Kate said. "Look!" She pointed.

The mutt sat by the Kenworth as if it had found a home. But it did not wag its tail at their approach.

Barry looked at the animal. It was a mixed breed but with the Husky in it predominant. He decided that somewhere down the line, the animal's ancestors had bred with either wolves or coyotes. Barry settled on wolves, for the dog still maintained the Husky markings, but with the eyes and snout of a wolf.

Kate knelt down and held out her hands. "Come on, boy," she urged.

The animal came to her, allowing her to pet him.

"What's that on his collar?" Barry asked.

Kate loosened the string holding the worn piece of paper. "A note," she said. She opened the folded paper and read aloud. "Goddamn dog bites. You find him, you can have the son of a bitch. He's two years old. Shots are due in the fall. I called him Dog."

31

Barry knew there was no use trying to dissuade Kate. Dog had found a home.

"Keep him on the floor until we can find a place to bathe him," Barry said. "He's got fleas."

Kate ignored that and put him in the sleeper.

"Thanks," Barry said dryly.

Swamp Wolf and Cajun had said nothing about Dog. If Barry and Kate wanted fleas, that was their business.

At a small town just outside Arizona, they stopped at a vet's place and had Dog bathed. Dog tolerated it without making a fuss.

"Got some wolf in him," the vet observed. "And a mean look about him. I oughta muzzle him, but he seems to be taking the bath in stride."

Dog was weighed. Sixty-five pounds.

Kate bought a case of Alpo, a water pan, and a food dish. Dog jumped up on the bunk and settled right in.

"I think he belonged to a trucker," Kate said. "He seems to know his way around a cab."

"I wonder if he can drive?" Barry asked.

Dog shifted his cold yellow eyes toward Barry.

"Just kidding," Barry told him.

Barry stopped a half-dozen places looking for a dune buggy. He struck out everywhere he looked. He gave up on the dune buggy idea and bought several motorcycles—dirt bikes, used, but in good condition. Barry and Kate tied them down inside the trailer and headed out for the scheduled rendezvous. When one was asleep in the bunk, Dog would sit in the empty seat, looking around, or lie down on the floor and sleep.

They pulled into the rendezvous spot and linked up with the others. Barry could tell by the grins on their faces they had scored well with the supplies.

"It's a short run to where we're going," he told them. "About a two-and-a-half-hour drive. We're going to hit them fast and hard. We free the inmates, then burn the goddamned place to the ground. After Texas, we'll probably be expected, so heads up, people. Let's roll!"

But they weren't expected. The guards had not been beefed up at all; if anything, security here was even worse than back in Texas.

And the cells and cages and laboratory were deserted.

"What the hell? . . ." Barry questioned aloud.

"Do we burn it?" Slim asked.

"To the ground." Barry walked to what appeared to him to be the man in charge. "The inmates—what happened to them?"

"A truck came early this morning," the man replied. "Took them away. I don't know where."

Barry believed him. He knew from experience that most people, when they lie, make up elaborate stories, easy to trip up. For as Twain said, no man has a good enough memory to be a successful liar.

"And you just let them?"

"They had government orders. If you'll accompany me to my office, I'll show you my copy."

"I'd like to see them."

Barry's hand shook slightly as he read the orders. It was no less than a presidential order. In it were the facilities named to be closed. Twelve of them. But the facility in Texas has been crossed out.

It was signed by the President of the United States.

"Have you tried to verify this?" Barry asked.

"Yes. I've called all the other CSS stations. The trucks began arriving early last night. This . . . particular part of the CSS is concluded, I suppose."

"You suppose? Aren't you glad it's over?"

"Not particularly. I rather enjoyed my work."

Barry came close to hitting him. He steadied himself and cooled down. "What about the animals?"

"Eh? Oh, they were destroyed. Pity, too. We had some good work going with some of them."

Barry walked outside before he jacked the guy's jaw. He ordered his people back to their trucks.

"What's up, boss?" Slim asked.

"It's over."

"Over?"

Barry explained, as much as he could. "There is still a lot I don't know, but I suppose we'll find out someday. Slim, you're free to walk. I'll call my attorney and have him destroy that confession."

Slim grinned. "How 'bout a job drivin' for Rivers Trucking?"

"You got that." Barry stuck out his hand and Slim shook it.

"Let's go home," Kate said.

Beer Butt honked his air horns. "Let them truckers *roll!*"

John Weston sat across from the President of the United States in the den at Camp David, or, as it is now listed, Camp 3. "Mr. President, with all due respect, sir. I have to say, with my badge in my hand, ready to turn it in . . . you fucked it all up!"

The President laughed. "Oh, I think not, John. When I learned of those damnable experiment stations, I was sick . . . really, physically sick. I signed the order as quickly as possible. I . . . didn't know you were setting up this Barry Rivers to take a fall for us."

"He's ideal, sir!" Weston said quickly. He looked at Jackson for support. The Treasury man nodded his agreement.

"I don't like a good man being treated in such a manner," the President said. "I think the . . . plan we spoke of is a good one. A workable one. But not starting out the way you planned. Not . . . well, quite like you planned."

The President stood up and stretched, walked to a window, gazing out. "The President of the United States must make, from time to time, some very difficult decisions. Ones that he might find personally repugnant. Where is this Barry Rivers right now?"

"Probably still in Arizona, getting ready to head back to New Orleans."

"For the good of the nation," the President muttered. "Keep that in mind always, partner."

"Beg pardon, sir?" Jackson said, leaning forward.

The President turned away from the window. "Nothing. Just talking to myself. In Arizona, you say. Two full days back to New Orleans—lovely city. Two or three days there, getting everything back shipshape with his trucking company. Then two or three days back to his offices. That about the way you boys figure it?"

They did. Both of them wondering what in the hell The Man had in mind.

"A full week." He sighed. "I'm going to let the chips fall where they may, gentlemen." He looked up at the ceiling, talking to a lamp fixture. "About twelve to fifteen agents of various departments have not shown up for work. So I'm told. And Mr. Jack Morris has been rather edgy lately; again, so I'm told. Whoever Jack Morris is," he added very quickly.

John Weston and Jackson relaxed, slight smiles in place. The Man was going to do it, but do it his way.

The President changed personalities as swiftly as a striking snake, fixing steely eyes on the top agents of their respective departments. A lot of press people mistakenly believed this President was not too sharp. Those who came in close contact with him in his decision making knew only too well how wrong the press types were. Not only was he extremely intelligent, but tough as leather.

"I don't want anything happening to innocent people," the President said. "Women, children, the elderly . . . any of those aforementioned who might be related to Barry Rivers, had better be, in two hours, covered like a blanket." He glanced at his watch, then pointed to a bank of phones. "You both have five minutes to make your calls. Do it!"

That done, the men settled down in their chairs before the desk.

"Set up long-term SST contracts with Rivers Trucking."

Both men knew better than to make notes. They would commit everything to memory.

"I don't care what they haul; they can haul dried cat shit if that's all that's available. But I want Barry's friends back on the road, fully armed with SST papers. Understood?"

Weston and Jackson understood.

"This Morris fellow . . . his phones are tapped, I take it?"

"Yes, sir."

"I would rather he think Barry Rivers is dead. Is that possible?"

"I . . . don't know, sir," Weston said. "We can probably keep both parties from making contact with each other."

"That will do. Do it."

"Uh . . . sir," Jackson said. "Exactly what do you have in mind?"

"It will develop, or it will not," the President said.

"Yes, sir."

Weston smiled. "You're going to want any and all warrants against Rivers squashed, right, sir?"

"That is correct."

"Until he kills Jack Morris, that is," Weston said, speaking around his smile.

"*If* he kills the man," the President corrected.

"Why not just approach him, sir?" Jackson asked. "I think Rivers would do it."

"I would prefer to have . . . insurance. Thank you, gentlemen. Let's get busy."

Weston and Jackson left. The President's chief adviser entered the room and sat down.

"You get it all on tape?" The President asked.

"Yes."

"Delete any reference to me."

"Yes, sir."

"The Dog," the President muttered. "I like it."

"Why not have something like, oh, Strike Force One?" the adviser suggested.

"Fuck Strike Force One," the President said. "Just call him The Dog."

32

"It's kind of . . . kind of, what am I trying to say, Barry?" Kate asked. "A downer, I guess."

"Anticlimactic."

She grinned at him. "Smartass!"

Barry did not return her smile. "It isn't over, Kate."

"What do you mean?"

"Too easy. Things like this don't end with a whimper, they end with a bang. But this operation just rolled over soundlessly."

"There is still your partner to think about," she reminded him.

"I'm not worried about Jack. It was too easy, Kate. Weston, Jackson, Borman, Stemke, Jennings, the whole bunch of them. They knew what I was doing; why do I get this feeling they *wanted* me to get caught?"

"I seen a movie like that one time. Something about a double-double-cross."

"How about a double-setup, Kate?"

"But why would the government want to set you up?"

He sighed. "I don't know. But I've got a bad feeling in my guts, honey."

"Maybe it's all them greasy hamburgers you been eatin'?" she said, then laughed.

Barry laughed with her.

But he laughed only to conceal his doubts from her.

The trip back to New Orleans was uneventful. And they paid absolutely no attention to driving time, making the run straight through. Back in his office, he dialed Fabrello's residence. The man had just returned from overseas, after learning there were no warrants out for him.

But he was very cool.

"What's wrong, Ted?" Barry asked. "Hell, it's over, finally."

"This will be our last communication, Barry," the capo said. "From now on all bets are off. I ain't plannin' no moves against your company—for as long as you have it, that is—but we ain't friends no more, understood?"

"No, I don't. Would you like to explain that, Ted?"

"I can't," the capo admitted. "Both our phones is bugged. Today, I'm changin' my number. You don't get the new number." He sighed deeply. "Goddamn, I don't want you for my enemy. You're one of them high-principled people, and you might get it into your head to come after me. I wouldn't like that."

"Ted, will you please tell me what in the hell you're talking about?"

But he was speaking into a dead phone.

He slowly replaced the receiver. "Curious," he muttered. "Very, very odd."

He told his father about the odd conversation with Fabrello.

"That is odd," Big Joe said. "What do you make of it, boy?"

"Nothing. I don't know. Hell!" he said, waving a hand. "Maybe I'm just becoming paranoid. Let's change the subject; get back to the trucking business."

"Fine with me." But the elder Rivers could see his son was still upset.

Barry handed back control of the company to his father, formally resigning his posts.

"How's it feel to be unemployed, boy?" Big Joe kidded him.

Kate was busy packing her things and making arrangements to sell her trailer, preparing to move to Maryland and settle down.

Dog was with her, watching her.

Kate had insisted that Barry buy a camper shell for his pickup, so Dog would be more comfortable on the trip.

"Jesus!" Barry said. "You treat him better than you would one of our kids."

"We're gonna have to get to work on that, too," she said, smiling.

"Now that's the kind of work I like!"

They pulled out on the third morning back in New Orleans, heading north.

They had just crossed the line into Virginia, on the interstate, when Barry felt the first hint of suspicion overtake him. He checked his mirrors. Had that car been following them? He thought so. He thought that was the car that followed them out of New Orleans. Yesterday the car had been green. All day. Now there was that blue car. Again.

It came up fast. Barry tensed. The car passed them and rolled out of sight.

Barry relaxed.

He pulled into a motel a few minutes later, just at dusk, checking in for the night.

The next morning, after breakfast, they packed up, tossing the luggage in the back, under the camper shell. Kate got behind the wheel.

Dog barked.

"Maybe he wants to go for a walk," Kate said. "You take him. I'll warm up the truck."

"Come on, Dog," Barry said. "Time for you to do your business."

Barry and Dog walked across the concrete to the grassy area. While Dog ran and sniffed, looking for just the right spot to mark, Barry heard the pickup's engine turn over, the motor firing. White-hot heat struck him hard, just as a tremendous sound wave knocked him sprawling to the ground. Out of shocked eyes, he saw Dog rolling over and over on the ground. He could just hear the sounds of falling debris; chunks of metal and brick and glass hitting the earth.

He felt a warm stickiness running down his face. Blood.

He was burning; his shirt was on fire.

But where was the pain?

He tried to roll over. Could not. None of his extremities would obey commands from his brain. Red tinged with a strange blackness began enveloping him as the pain reached him.

Dog was barking.

"Kate!" he yelled, but her name was only a whisper coming out of his mouth.

And then he knew nothing as a cold hand touched him lightly with bony fingers.

* * *

"He's dead!" Jack Morris almost screamed the words over the phone. "The Green Beret bastard is finally dead."

Paul Rivers sighed as a great weight was lifted from him. "You're sure he's dead?"

"Everyone is dead. Barry, Kate, even that stupid dog they found."

"Now we can move against the old man."

"All in time, Paul. First we grieve; put on a very convincing sackcloth-and-ashes bit."

"Yes. You're right, of course. I'll see you at the funeral."

"Oh, yes. Certainly."

Both men were laughing as they hung up.

33

Barry opened his eyes, but he could not make them focus. He blinked several times. His throat felt raw; like something was stuck there. He finally realized it was a tube. One in his nose, too. His arms . . . he couldn't move them.

He almost panicked, then steeled his emotions.

His eyes began to focus. A hospital room. His arms were strapped down because he had needles in both arms.

But he was alive.

Big deal. Shit! he couldn't move.

Worse than that, he could not remember anything. Why was he here? What happened?

He knew he was not in the hospital in Saigon. He'd been there; this wasn't it.

A barking dog. He remembered that. But why would he remember that?

Dog!

Kate!

He strained against his bonds. But he was very weak. He tried to yell. He managed a croaking sound.

Goddamn tube.

He cut his eyes as the door opened. A nurse looked at him looking at her. Her eyes widened. She spoke sharply to someone in the hall. She was a military nurse, Barry noted. Captain. Air Force or Army, he wasn't sure.

Two men quickly entered the room.

"Whathsiginon?" Barry mumbled, knowing the words made no sense.

"Don't try to talk," one of the men said. He turned to the nurse. "Get the tube out of his throat."

And that was unpleasant.

His arms were freed from the restraints. The needles were removed. The tube in his nose was removed.

"How do you feel, Mr. Rivers?" the second man asked. "And I understand that is a very foolish question."

"Like I've been rode hard and put up wet." Barry managed to push the words out of a very parched throat.

"Have a sip of water."

Barry sipped the water. Felt good. Eased the dryness in his throat. "I'm hungry as hell."

"Soup," the doctor ordered.

The doctors poked him, prodded him, checked his blood pressure and heart, and grunted several times.

"Kate?" Barry asked several times.

A third man entered the room. Barry looked at him and knew him for what he was. A shrink. He'd seen too many of them during his years in Special Forces.

"Somebody better fucking tell me something!" Barry said.

"Take it easy, Barry," the shrink said. "Don't get yourself agitated. What day is it?"

Barry told him the day, month, and year.

"You've got the year right," a doctor said. "You're a bit off on the others."

Barry cut his eyes to the draped windows. "Let me see outside."

The leaves on the trees were changing; bushes and shrubs were beginning to take on a dry, brittle look. Barry glanced back at the doctors.

"Fall," he said.

"Yes. You've been in a coma for several months, Barry."

Barry sighed. "I have a headache."

Aspirin was ordered.

"Kate?" Barry asked.

"She's dead, Barry," the shrink told him.

It came as no surprise. Then everything came rushing back, his memory banks emptying. Barry was silent for several moments, digesting and reviewing the events of months past. "Where am I?"

"Fort Drum."

New York State. "Where is Kate . . . buried?" He stumbled over the word.

"New Orleans."

Barry drank his soup, took his aspirin, and asked for more soup. It was brought to him. But surprisingly, he could not finish the bowl of soup.

"Your stomach has shrunk. It won't take long for you to get back to normal."

"Your dog is outside playing," one of the doctors informed him. "He bites," he added. "What is his name?"

"Dog." He thought for a moment. "He's due for his shots." He remembered the note; Kate reading it.

"We'll take care of it."

"My truck blew up?"

"Yes."

"No way anyone could have put a bomb under the hood. It would have set off an alarm."

"It was a vibration bomb, Barry. You're familiar with the type."

"Yes."

"You rest for a while, Barry. We'll be back to see you."

With the room darkened, Barry turned his head away from the door and wept. Silently. When he had no more tears to cry, he wiped his eyes and let waves of revenge feelings sweep over him. He looked up at the ceiling.

"I'll find you," he whispered. "Whoever you are, wherever you are, I'll track you down and I'll kill you."

Fall melted into winter and snow blanketed the hospital grounds. Barry underwent intensive therapy, both mentally and physically. He had been badly burned, and was forced to undergo several operations. Once more on his feet, he began exercising, slowly at first, then picking up the pace. He regained his weight, and, working out in the gym, regained his strength and timing.

One side of his face had been completely reworked, altering his appearance. His nose had been smashed. It was rebuilt and reshaped.

He was staying in a guest cottage on the base, living quietly alone, with Dog.

And his memories.

His days were filled with exercise and sessions with the shrinks. The nights were haunted with dreams of Kate.

And Barry Rivers learned he was dead and buried. Buried beside Kate in New Orleans.

He had stared at the shrink. *"What?"* he'd blurted.

"You're dead, Mr. Rivers. Your package has been pulled at Central Records; your Social Security number retired. Your life insurance paid off. Your company was purchased by Jack Morris. You no longer exist."

34

Barry left the hospital grounds for the first time in April. He looked much older than his years; sometime during his coma, gray had crept into his hair, salt-and-peppering it. The operations had changed his looks forever. Even Dog looked older. He was no longer the playful mutt he and Kate had found in the parking lot.

Kate.

Barry tried to keep her face out of the light of inner vision as much as possible. Sometimes it worked, sometimes it didn't.

Barry walked toward a midnight-blue Kenworth parked across from the hospital grounds. He opened the door, and Dog jumped up and down and ran around in circles, ready to go. Barry helped him into the rig and climbed in after him, settling down behind the wheel. He picked up the package lying on the console.

His new life was contained within the thick envelope.

New York State driver's license. Barry Rivera. The address was real, but Barry had never seen the place.

The Kenworth was his home. From now on. Forever.

He checked his credit cards. Several dozen of them. Visa, MasterCard, American Express, all sorts of gas cards.

Dog spoke to him in that funny Husky way. Kate had called it doggy talk.

"You ready to roll, Dog?"

Dog was ready.

Barry pulled out and away from the military reservation, picked up Interstate 81 at Watertown, and pointed the big snout of the Kenworth south. He would be running empty down to Andrews AFB, just outside Washington. There he was to pick up a load. He didn't know what it was or where he was taking it.

Just that he would be traveling alone. The only SST rig on the road with only one driver. Dog and Dog.

It had taken some doing. But Barry had remained firm with the government men he'd met at the hospital cottage. That was the only way he'd play their game.

They had finally, reluctantly, agreed.

He had plenty of time before he picked up his load. There was someone he wanted to see in the Washington area.

As he drove the interstate system, he firmed up his plans and thought about his new life.

He had met the President. He had been impressed with the man. And he liked the man's bluntness.

"Country has gone to shit, Barry," the man had said. "We're slowly bringing the country back to dead center, but that won't be fully accomplished in my lifetime. But you might be able to help. You interested?"

"Do I have a choice?"

"Yes." The man was honest. "At first I was going to hold criminal charges over your head. But I soon rejected that. I was not comfortable with it. You hear me out. Then, if you're not interested, we suddenly locate you in a hospital, where you've been in a coma for months. You're back to life once more."

"Either way it goes, Mr. President, I'm going to kill Jack Morris."

The President's smile was thin. "Then you'd better saddle up and ride with us, Barry."

"Call me Dog."

The President had left an hour later.

Barry left his truck at Andrews AFB, Dog with it lying under the trailer, growling menacingly when anyone got too close.

The APs said they'd keep him fed and watered.

"He bites," Barry warned the APs.

"No shit?" one of them said, eyeballing Dog.

Barry stood outside the Justice building, arriving there just before noon. Linda was in the crowd leaving for lunch, buying it or brown-bagging it, to eat in the nearby park. She looked right at him, this rough-looking man dressed in boots and jeans and western denim shirt.

Not one trace of recognition passed over her face.

Barry turned away and walked to a rent-a-car place. He rented a small car and drove to his old offices, driving past them to a service station about a half-mile away. He used the pay phone to call his old office, asking for Maggie.

She was no longer employed there, he was informed.

I'm sorry to hear that. I'm an old friend. Is she ill?

No. She quit.

The person hung up.

He drove back past the office, just in time to see lard-assed Jack leaving. He had not changed his habits. He still left for lunch at one-thirty. Barry followed him. Driving with one hand, he opened a brown paper sack on the seat beside him, taking out a .22 caliber semiautomatic pistol, tapped for silencer, the stubby noise suppressor screwed on. Jack was in the far right lane, Barry in the lane next to him. Both drivers' side windows were lowered.

"You're on your own, Dog." The President's words returned to him as they approached a traffic light. "You are judge, jury, and executioner. You could very easily get out of control. If that happens, you won't live twenty-four more hours. Do you understand?"

"Perfectly."

"You will never see me again," the President told him. "Your contact is Jackson or Weston. I do not know you. I never heard of you. I never want to hear from you."

"Fine with me."

The light changed to red. Barry pulled up beside Jack. Jack looked up. His face looked dissipated. Barry smiled as he checked the mirrors. No other vehicle was close.

"Hello, fat-ass!" Barry said.

"What!" Jack said, his eyes widening as Barry lifted the silenced pistol.

"Goddamned scum-suckin' motherfucker!" Barry said, then pulled the trigger.

The pistol huffed four times, all four slugs taking Jack in the face. One slug entered his left eye and exited out the back of his head.

The light changed to green. Barry drove away. Jack's blood was soaking into the seat of his car.

Barry drove back into D.C. and had a quiet lunch. He turned the car back in and returned to Andrews. He picked up his orders and boosted Dog up into the cab. He was rolling through Virginia at dusk.

"Anywhere there is trouble is where you'll go, Dog." The President's words rang in his head. "You might be sent there, you might decide to go on your own. Most of the time, it will be up to you."

"Fine."

"You won't reconsider and have a partner?"

"I have a partner."

"Who?"

"Dog."

He pulled into Baton Rouge and made a phone call.

"I am sorry," the woman's voice said. "But Paul is very ill."

"I'm sorry to hear that," Barry said. "Tell him an old . . . friend called, will you?"

"You don't know about Paul?"

"I don't understand. What about Paul?"

"He's in Glenlake." Paul's wife hung up.

Barry drove to the private mental hospital. He met with the director and identified himself as an old family friend of Paul Rivers.

"Very tragic case, Mister . . . ah? . . ."

"Rivera. Paul was my attorney some time back. Really helped me out of a bad jam I was in."

"Of course. Paul was truly a fine, fine man."

"Was? Is he dead?"

"In a manner of speaking. I shall put this in layman's language, Mr. Rivera. Paul Rivers is insane. He will never leave Glenlake."

"Could I see him?"

The director hesitated. "Well, it's . . . oh, I suppose so. Of course, he won't know you."

"Of course."

Paul Rivers sat in a rubber room, padded for his own protection. He slobbered and babbled and messed on himself.

"When did this happen?"

"About six months ago. We don't know where he got the LSD. He'd been to Washington, D.C., for some kind of business meeting."

Good ol' lard-assed Jack had struck again. But Jack's days at the plate were over.

"There is no hope for him?" Barry asked. "None at all?"

"None at all. His mind is destroyed."

Barry again looked at his brother. Paul blew spit bubbles at him, then squatted and shit on the floor.

35

Barry off-loaded at Fork Polk. There, he was handed a sealed envelope.

ST. LOUIS.

That was it. Barry wondered what he'd find in St. Louis.

Only one way to find out, he thought, climbing back into his rig.

"You ready, Dog?" he asked.

Dog growled.

Barry rolled out.

"It could be government work." The President's words again came to him. "You might be asked to give up your life. Do you fully understand?"

Barry thought of Kate.

"I understand."

He angled toward the northeast, crossing the river at Natchez, heading for the interstate at Brookhaven. Heading for the unknown.

"You in the Kenworth," his CB cracked. "You got a handle?"

"Dog," Barry came back. "Just Dog."

William W. Johnstone
The *Mountain Man* Series

<u>BOOK YOUR PLACE ON OUR WEBSITE</u> <u>AND MAKE THE</u> <u>READING CONNECTION!</u>

We've created a customized website just for our very special readers, where you can get the inside scoop on everything that's going on with Zebra, Pinnacle and Kensington books.

When you come online, you'll have the exciting opportunity to:

• View covers of upcoming books

• Read sample chapters

• Learn about our future publishing schedule (listed by publication month *and author*)

• Find out when your favorite authors will be visiting a city near you

• Search for and order backlist books from our online catalog

• Check out author bios and background information

• Send e-mail to your favorite authors

• Meet the Kensington staff online

• Join us in weekly chats with authors, readers and other guests

• Get writing guidelines

• AND MUCH MORE!

Visit our website at
http://www.pinnaclebooks.com